SWEET RIVER HOLIDAY HOMECOMING

CHRISTMAS SEASHELLS AND SNOWFLAKES

KAY CORRELL

ZURA LU PUBLISHING LLC

This book is dedicated to our family's lovely Christmas traditions. Seeing traditions passed down from generation to generation. Sharing them with grandchildren. I hope each of you reading this book have a wonderful holiday season full of family, friendship, and joy.

ABOUT THIS BOOK

She came home to heal her father. She never expected to find her own heart on the line.

When ER nurse Tessa Grant rushes back to her hometown after her estranged father's stroke, she expects to find the same emotionally distant man she left behind fifteen years ago. Instead, she discovers her father has changed, and a mysterious stranger is living in her childhood home, helping her father. Beckett is frustratingly kind, impossibly steady, and somehow knows more about her father's daily life than she has in a decade.

Tessa plans to handle her father's recovery and escape back to Denver before Christmas. But as holiday lights twinkle in the picturesque mountain town of Sweet River Falls, the walls she's built begin to crumble.

Between helping with the town's Christmas festival, baking her mother's treasured cookie recipes, and witnessing the unexpected bond between her father and Beckett—a man with his own troubled past

—Tessa finds herself questioning everything she thought she knew about family, belonging, and where she truly fits.

As snow blankets the mountains and the town prepares for its Christmas Eve candlelight walk, Tessa discovers that healing comes in unexpected forms, second chances are worth fighting for, and sometimes the best gift is finding your way back home to family, to love, and to yourself.

A heartwarming Christmas story about forgiveness, finding home, and the families we choose that will leave you reaching for hot chocolate and believing in holiday magic long after the last page.

KAY'S BOOKS

Find more information on all my books at **_kaycorrell.com_**

Buy direct from Kay's Shop at **_shop.kaycorrell.com_**

COMFORT CROSSING ~ THE SERIES
The Shop on Main - Book One
The Memory Box - Book Two
The Christmas Cottage - A Holiday Novella (Book 2.5)
The Letter - Book Three
The Christmas Scarf - A Holiday Novella (Book 3.5)
The Magnolia Cafe - Book Four
The Unexpected Wedding - Book Five

The Wedding in the Grove - (a crossover short story

between series - with Josephine and Paul from The Letter.)

LIGHTHOUSE POINT ~ THE SERIES
Wish Upon a Shell - Book One
Wedding on the Beach - Book Two
Love at the Lighthouse - Book Three
Cottage near the Point - Book Four
Return to the Island - Book Five
Bungalow by the Bay - Book Six
Christmas Comes to Lighthouse Point - Book Seven

CHARMING INN ~ Return to Lighthouse Point
One Simple Wish - Book One
Two of a Kind - Book Two
Three Little Things - Book Three
Four Short Weeks - Book Four
Five Years or So - Book Five
Six Hours Away - Book Six
Charming Christmas - Book Seven

SWEET RIVER ~ THE SERIES
A Dream to Believe in - Book One
A Memory to Cherish - Book Two
A Song to Remember - Book Three
A Time to Forgive - Book Four
A Summer of Secrets - Book Five
A Moment in the Moonlight - Book Six

MOONBEAM BAY ~ THE SERIES

The Parker Women - Book One

The Parker Cafe - Book Two

A Heather Parker Original - Book Three

The Parker Family Secret - Book Four

Grace Parker's Peach Pie - Book Five

The Perks of Being a Parker - Book Six

BLUE HERON COTTAGES ~ THE SERIES

Memories of the Beach - Book One

Walks along the Shore - Book Two

Bookshop near the Coast - Book Three

Restaurant on the Wharf - Book Four

Lilacs by the Sea - Book Five

Flower Shop on Magnolia - Book Six

Christmas by the Bay - Book Seven

Sea Glass from the Past - Book Eight

MAGNOLIA KEY ~ THE SERIES

Saltwater Sunrise - Book One

Encore Echoes - Book Two

Coastal Candlelight - Book Three

Tidal Treasures - Book Four

Bayside Beginnings - Book Five

Seaside Sunshine - Book Six

Boardwalk Breezes - Book Seven

CHRISTMAS SEASHELLS AND SNOWFLAKES

Seaside Christmas Wishes

Sweet River Holiday Homecoming

WIND CHIME BEACH ~ A stand-alone novel

INDIGO BAY ~

Sweet Days by the Bay - Kay's Complete Collection
of stories in the Indigo Bay series

Sign up for my newsletter at my website *kaycorrell.com*
to make sure you don't miss any new releases or
sales.

CHAPTER 1

THE LAST PERSON Tessa Grant expected to see in the ER on a busy Friday night was her father's neighbor, Fran Wilkins, with her silver hair twisted into a messy bun and worry lines creasing her forehead. But there she stood, clutching her phone in the waiting room, looking as out of place in Denver as a snowman in July.

"He's stable," Fran said, her voice crackling like autumn leaves. "But he asked for you. First time in years, Tessa."

The words hit like a cardiac arrest. Sudden, jarring, demanding immediate attention. Tessa's fingers tightened into a fist beneath the harsh fluorescent lights. Eighteen hours into her shift, and the controlled chaos of the emergency room suddenly felt like the easier option.

"I can't just—" The excuse died on her lips.

What would she say? That she couldn't leave because of the holiday staffing shortage? That she hadn't spoken more than ten sentences to her father in the last decade? That the thought of returning to Sweet River Falls made her lungs constrict like an asthma attack?

Fran had watched Tessa grow up and witnessed the slow fracturing of the Grant family. The woman's knowing eyes cut through her defenses. "Minor stroke, the doctor said. But minor doesn't mean nothing, does it? Not at his age."

At his age. The words landed with surprising punch. When had Stan Grant become old? In Tessa's mind, he was perpetually fifty-something, straight-backed and stern-faced, disappointment etched into the lines around his mouth.

"I'll need to talk to my supervisor," she said finally, the words emerging clinical and detached. She used her professional voice, the one that carried her through gunshot wounds and panicked patients without revealing the human beneath the scrubs. "I'll leave after my shift."

Four hours later, she was driving through darkness on I-70, her hastily packed duffel bag tossed in the back seat of her Subaru. The highway stretched before her like a black ribbon, snow beginning to dust the shoulders. Her eyes burned from exhaustion, but her mind was too wired for sleep. She'd worked twenty hours straight before starting this drive in a familiar pattern of pushing herself past reasonable limits.

The mountains loomed larger as she approached, silent guardians that had watched her leave all those years ago. She'd fled Sweet River Falls like it was a burning building, grabbing only what she could carry. Denver had been far enough to escape but close enough that she could still tell herself she hadn't completely abandoned her father. Close enough that she could have visited if either of them had really wanted it.

She'd come back exactly twice. Once for Fran's husband's funeral seven years ago, and once, briefly, when her father had pneumonia. On the second trip, she'd kept her nurse's scrubs on like armor and focused on medical needs rather than the emotional wounds that never seemed to heal properly.

The highway signs for Sweet River Falls appeared, and she gripped the steering wheel tighter. She checked her watch. 6:30 AM. What a homecoming.

The town emerged from the darkness like a holiday postcard. Twinkling lights were strung across Main Street, wreaths hung on every lamp-post, and a dusting of fresh snow made everything look impossibly clean. She drove slowly, trying to reorient herself. Not much had changed. There was a new clothing store she didn't recognize, and the candy store had a new name, but the bones of the place remained stubbornly the same.

She turned onto Cedar Lane as muscle memory guided her to the small cottage where she'd grown up. It looked smaller than she remembered, nestled between towering pines. A single lamp glowed in the front window, and someone had strung white Christmas lights along the eaves. Strange, because her father had never bothered with Christmas decorations after her mother died.

She sat in her idling car, studying the house like it was a patient chart. The front steps had been recently shoveled. A wreath hung on the door. It was simple but definitely not something her father would have put up himself. Someone was helping him. Fran, probably.

With a deep breath, she grabbed her bag and medical kit and stepped out into the cold. The mountain air was sharper and cleaner than Denver's, carrying the scent of pine and smoke from a fireplace. Her boots crunched in the fresh snow as she made her way to the front door.

She had a key. She'd never returned it. But it somehow felt wrong to use it after so long. Instead, she knocked softly, not wanting to startle her father if he was sleeping.

No answer.

She knocked again, a little harder.

The porch light flicked on, and she stepped

back, straightening her shoulders and smoothing her hair in an automatic response ingrained from childhood. Be presentable. Stand up straight. Don't show weakness.

But when the door opened, it wasn't her father's face that greeted her. Instead, a tall man with watchful gray-blue eyes and tousled dark blond hair stood in the doorway, wearing flannel pajama pants and a thermal Henley shirt. He regarded her with cautious curiosity, neither welcoming nor hostile.

"Can I help you?" His voice was deep and quiet, with the careful enunciation of someone who measured his words before speaking them.

She blinked, momentarily thrown off balance. "I'm here to see Stan Grant." She slipped her professional voice back into place. "I'm his daughter."

Something shifted in the man's expression. It was recognition, maybe, or surprise. He stepped back, opening the door wider. "Tessa. I didn't know you were coming. I'm Beckett." He held out a hand, then seemed to think better of it, letting it fall back to his side. "Come in. Your dad's asleep, but he's been doing okay. Better than yesterday."

She stepped into the house, the familiar smell of it hitting her with unexpected force. The living room was mostly as she remembered it. The same worn leather sofa along the far wall, the bookshelf filled with her father's fishing magazines and mystery novels, and the stone fireplace where a small fire flickered.

But there were differences, too. A quilt she didn't recognize was draped over the back of the sofa. A different coffee table. And on the mantel, photos she'd never seen before. They looked to be more recent ones of her father with people she didn't know.

She set down her bag and turned to face the stranger in her childhood home. "I'm sorry, but who exactly are you? And why are you in my father's house at six in the morning?"

The man—Beckett, wasn't it—didn't flinch at her direct question. Instead, he rubbed a hand over the stubble on his jaw, a gesture that seemed more thoughtful than nervous.

He shrugged. "I live here. Have for about six months now. I help your dad with the house, yard work, that sort of thing." He paused, watching her face carefully. "I'm part of a reentry program through Grace Chapel. Room and board in exchange for help around the place."

Reentry program. The words hung in the air between them. Her brain quickly connected the dots. Reentry meant he was coming back from somewhere. Prison, most likely. Her eyes flicked to his hands, noting the calluses, to his face, taking in the faint scar above his brow, to his posture, which remained carefully non-threatening.

A quiet anger began to simmer beneath her exhaustion. Her father had let a stranger—*an ex-con at that*—move into their home without so much as mentioning it to her. She'd spoken to him on the phone just last month. Okay, maybe it had been two months ago. Maybe three. It had been a stilted five-minute conversation about nothing important, and he hadn't thought to mention that he had a roommate.

"I see," she said, her voice cooler than the December air outside. "And where is my father now?"

Beckett motioned toward the hallway. "His bedroom. The doctor wants him to rest as much as possible. Your room's still there, though. Doesn't look like he ever changed it."

Your room. The words caught her off guard. She hadn't thought of that bedroom as hers in years. It was a museum exhibit of her teenage self, a self she barely recognized anymore.

"I'd like to see him." She reached for her medical kit.

"He's on some pretty strong sleep medication. The doctor said not to wake him unless necessary. Later morning would be better. I can show you to your room, if you'd like." His voice remained neutral, but there was a quiet firmness to it.

She wanted to argue and assert her authority as both a medical professional and a daughter. But the exhaustion of her shift and the long drive crashed over her in waves. Her clinical judgment, the one thing she could always rely on, told her that Beckett was right. Waking her father now wouldn't help anyone.

"Fine," she conceded, picking up her bag again. "But I want a full rundown of his condition, medications, and doctor's instructions."

Beckett nodded, no surprise or offense registering on his face. "Of course. I've got it all written down in the kitchen. His follow-up appointment is scheduled for the 27th." He turned toward the hallway, then paused, glancing back at her. "It's good you came. He'll be glad to see you."

The simple statement, delivered without judgment or expectation, somehow made the knot inside her tighten. She followed Beckett down the familiar hallway, past her father's closed door, to the room at the end. Her room, apparently untouched in her decade-long absence.

He stepped aside, allowing her to enter first. "Bathroom's stocked with fresh towels. Let me know if you need anything else."

She nodded stiffly, too tired for proper gratitude, too unsettled for politeness. "Thank you," she managed, but the words came out more clipped than she intended.

He dipped his head in a small nod and retreated, his footsteps quiet on the hardwood floor.

Alone in her childhood bedroom, she set down her bags and surveyed the space. Pale blue walls, faded posters of mountains and medical diagrams, and a bookshelf still lined with her old textbooks and paperbacks. The twin bed with its patchwork quilt that her grandmother had made. Everything was exactly as she'd left it, like a time capsule from another life.

She sat heavily on the edge of the bed, the familiar creak of the springs a ghost from her past. Outside, snow continued to fall, coating Sweet River Falls in silent white. Morning was dawning in a town she'd escaped, in a house now shared with a stranger, with her estranged father sleeping down the hall.

She pressed the heels of her hands against her burning eyes. She'd come to care for her father and be the nurse she'd been trained to be. She could do this. Clinical, professional, detached. Just another case to manage before returning to her real life.

But as she lay down on her childhood bed, still fully clothed, her homecoming settled over her like the snow outside. Quiet. Persistent. And impossible to ignore.

CHAPTER 2

Tessa woke with a jolt, her eyes flying open to unfamiliar shadows on the ceiling. No, not unfamiliar. Just forgotten. The glow-in-the-dark stars she'd stuck there as a child had long since lost their luminescence, but their outlines remained, faint ghosts of constellations past.

Her childhood bedroom. Sweet River Falls. Her father.

The events of the previous night came rushing back as she pushed herself upright, wincing at the stiffness in her neck. She'd fallen asleep fully clothed, her body finally surrendering after the marathon ER shift and the long drive through the mountains. Sunlight streamed through the faded blue curtains in a warm glow that felt both familiar and strange.

She checked her watch. 10:47 AM.

She never slept this late. Not even after night shifts. The realization made her push back the quilt and stand, her body protesting every movement. Her clothes were hopelessly wrinkled, and her mouth felt like it was stuffed with cotton.

Her duffel bag sat untouched where she'd dropped it. She rummaged through it, grateful that she'd had the presence of mind to pack a few essentials before leaving Denver. Clean clothes. Toothbrush. Basic toiletries. She'd packed in autopilot, the same way she prepared her go-bag for disaster relief work.

The bathroom was directly across the hall. She opened the door cautiously, half-expecting to find it occupied. It was empty, but not unchanged. The shower curtain was new, a simple navy blue instead of the sailing-themed one her father had kept for decades. A man's razor sat on the edge of the sink. Beckett's, obviously. At least he hung up his towel.

She would be sharing this bathroom with Beckett. The thought was oddly intimate, considering she'd just met the man. She closed the door and turned on the shower, letting the water run hot while she examined her reflection in the mirror.

Dark circles shadowed her eyes. Her chestnut hair had mostly escaped its bun, tendrils framing her face in a way that looked less artfully messy and more like she'd been dragged backward through a hedge. She looked every bit as exhausted as she felt.

The shower helped, washing away the hospital antiseptic smell that always seemed to cling to her skin after long shifts. She dressed quickly in clean jeans and a soft flannel shirt, twisting her damp hair into a fresh bun at the nape of her neck. No makeup. She hadn't bothered to pack any.

Voices drifted down the hallway as she emerged from the bathroom. She heard low murmurs and the occasional clink of silverware against plates. She followed the sounds to the kitchen, pausing at the threshold to take in the scene.

Her father sat at the small oak table by the window, a newspaper spread out before him and a mug of coffee at his elbow. A cane leaned against his chair. He looked smaller somehow, his shoulders slightly stooped, and his hair was thinner and whiter than she remembered. But his eyes, when he glanced up and saw her, were clear and sharp as ever.

Beckett stood at the stove, his back to her, flipping what looked like pancakes. He wore worn jeans and a faded thermal shirt. His movements were efficient and practiced. The kitchen smelled of coffee and maple syrup, homey scents that felt incongruous with the tension that swirled through the room.

"Well, you finally decided to join us." Her father folded his newspaper

Not, "good morning." Not, "it's good to see you." Just a pointed comment about her sleeping late. Some things never changed. "Good morning. How are you feeling?" She ignored his tone and moved into the kitchen, stopping a few feet from the table.

"Like I'm being asked how I'm feeling by everyone who walks through the door. Sit down. Beckett's making enough pancakes to feed an army." He motioned to the empty chair across from him.

"Just trying to use up the batter," Beckett said quietly, not turning around. "Coffee's fresh if you want some, Tessa."

The casual use of her name caught her off guard. She moved to the cabinet where the mugs had always been kept, finding them still in the same place. Some things remained constant, at least. She poured herself a cup, black, and finally approached the table.

"I'd like to check your vitals and go over your medication schedule," she said as she set down her coffee.

Stan Grant's jaw tightened. "I've already been poked and prodded by actual doctors, Tessa. I don't need my daughter playing nurse with me."

The familiar defensiveness rose in her chest. "I'm not playing anything. I am a nurse. And I'd like to understand exactly what happened and what your treatment plan is."

"Minor stroke. Taking medication. Resting." He

ticked the points off on his fingers. "There's your treatment plan."

Beckett approached with a plate stacked with pancakes, setting it in the center of the table. "Doctor said it was a TIA," he said, his voice matter-of-fact. "Transient ischemic attack. Blood pressure spiked, causing some temporary symptoms. No permanent damage." He moved back to the counter and returned with plates, silverware, and syrup. "He's on a blood thinner and something to control his blood pressure. I've got the schedule written down."

Her father shot Beckett a look that might have been annoyance, but Beckett seemed unperturbed as he took the seat between them.

"Thank you." She was surprised by the succinct, accurate summary. She turned back to her father. "Any lingering symptoms? Numbness? Difficulty speaking? Confusion?"

"Just difficulty dealing with unnecessary questions," Stan muttered, but he reached for the pancakes. "I'm fine, Tessa. Or I will be, once everyone stops treating me like I'm made of glass."

Beckett quietly served himself, then passed the platter to her. The three of them ate in silence for a moment, the only sounds the scrape of forks against plates and the ticking of the old clock on the wall.

"So, how long are you planning to stay?" her father finally asked.

The question hung in the air, loaded with unspoken meaning. *How long until you leave again? How long do I have to endure your presence? How long before you run back to Denver?*

"I took two weeks off," she answered, focusing on cutting her pancake into precise triangles. "I have some vacation time saved up."

Her father's eyebrows rose. "Two weeks? That's not necessary. I'll be back to normal in a few days."

"TIAs can be precursors to more serious strokes." She automatically slipped into her clinical voice. "You'll need to be monitored, and there will be follow-up appointments."

"Beckett's been driving me to appointments. Haven't you, Beck?"

Beck. The nickname surprised her. It suggested a familiarity, a comfort level between them that she hadn't expected.

"Happy to keep doing it, but having Tessa here will be good too." He glanced at her. "Extra pair of eyes."

"I don't need babysitters. Either of you," Stan grumbled.

"Stroke prevention is serious, Dad." The word "Dad" felt foreign on her tongue after so many years of avoiding direct address. "You need to make lifestyle changes. You need diet modifications, regular exercise, and stress reduction."

Beckett reached for his coffee. "Been working on

that already. We've been walking every morning. Started eating more fish, less red meat."

We. The casual way he included himself in her father's care routine made something twist in her stomach. It wasn't quite jealousy, but something adjacent to it. This stranger knew more about her father's daily life than she did.

"Well, that's... good," she managed. "The doctor probably recommended it."

"Actually, it was Beckett's idea," her father said, a hint of pride in his voice. "He's been reading up on heart health. Got me eating oatmeal for breakfast most days, though I drew the line at that green smoothie nonsense."

Beckett's mouth quirked in what might have been the beginning of a smile. "Still working on that one."

The easy rapport between them was unsettling. Her father had never been the type to form quick friendships or trust easily. Yet here he was, clearly comfortable with this quiet ex-con who'd moved into his house and apparently taken charge of his health regimen.

"So what exactly happened? When did you notice symptoms?" She steered the conversation back to medical territory where she felt more secure.

Her father sighed heavily. "Beckett found me. I don't remember much."

"He was in the workshop. He was having trouble finding words. I called 911."

"You were lucky he was here," she said quietly.

"Luck had nothing to do with it. Beckett's here because I invited him. Best decision I've made in years."

The comment stung more than it should have. She took a sip of coffee to hide her reaction.

"How long are you on leave from the hospital?" her father asked, changing the subject.

"I told you, two weeks." It was actually longer than that. What she didn't say was that she'd already planned to take time off. Last night was her last shift for a while. She also didn't mention the panic attack she'd had in the supply closet three weeks ago or the way her hands had started shaking during a routine procedure the week before that. Or how her supervisor had gently but firmly suggested she take some time off before she made a serious mistake.

The telephone rang, saving her from further explanation. Beckett rose to answer it, his movements fluid and unhurried.

"Grant residence." He listened for a moment, then held the phone out to her father. "It's Nora from the Lodge."

Stan took the phone. "Nora, hello." His voice softened noticeably. "Yes, I'm doing fine. No need to worry." He paused, listening. "Yes, she's here.

Arrived this morning." Another pause. "I'm sure she'd love to say hello. Hold on."

He held the phone out to her. "Nora Cassidy wants to talk to you."

She hesitated. Nora Cassidy. The name was familiar but distant, like a song she'd once known the words to.

"She owns Sweet River Lodge. You remember Nora," her father prompted.

Of course she did. Nora with the kind smile and the homemade cookies. Nora, who'd sent a hand-written sympathy card when her mother died. Nora, who'd tried to include Tessa in community events long after she'd stopped wanting to be included.

She took the phone reluctantly. "Hello?"

"Tessa Grant, is that really you? I was just telling your father how wonderful it is that you're home for Christmas. We've missed you around here." Nora's voice was warm and exactly as she remembered it.

Christmas. It was just a few weeks away. She never celebrated it anyway and typically volunteered for holiday shifts at the hospital to let colleagues with families have the time off.

"I'm just here to help my father recover. It's not really a holiday visit." She ignored how stiff she sounded… or at least tried to.

"Well, you're here, and it's the holidays, so I'd say that makes it a holiday visit. You simply must come to the lodge's Christmas festival. The whole town will be there. It'll be just like old times."

Just like old times. The last thing she wanted.

"I'll have to see how my father is feeling," she hedged.

"Oh, Stan's already promised to judge the gingerbread house competition. It's tradition! Beckett said he'd bring him." Nora's voice dropped to a conspiratorial whisper. "Such a nice young man, that Beckett. So helpful with your father. And not hard on the eyes either, if you don't mind my saying so."

She felt heat rise to her cheeks. "I really should go, Nora. It was nice talking to you."

"The festival starts at noon on Saturday. We'll save all three of you a seat at the Cassidy table." Nora's tone made it clear this wasn't a suggestion but a foregone conclusion. "And tell your father I'll be bringing some of my Christmas soup tomorrow."

She said goodbye and hung up, turning to find her father watching her with a knowing expression.

"Nora hasn't changed a bit. Still organizing everyone's social calendar," he said.

"You're judging a gingerbread house competition?" She couldn't keep the disbelief from her voice. Her father had never participated in town festivals, not since her mother died. Christmas had become just another day in the Grant household, marked only by their careful avoidance of anything that might trigger memories.

"I lost a bet with Jason Cassidy," he admitted. "But the lodge festival is good. They do it up right." He glanced at Beckett. "We're still planning to go, right?"

"If you're feeling up to it. The doctor said normal activities are fine as long as you're not overdoing it."

"I've been looking forward to it." Her father's words held more enthusiasm than she had heard from him in years. "They've got that new chalet all decorated, and Miss Judy's making her famous cinnamon rolls and cookies. Lots of cookies." He gave a quick look toward Beckett. "A few cookies won't hurt anything. Then it's back to all that healthy stuff you insist on."

She stared at him, trying to reconcile this man with the father she remembered. The one who'd packed away all the Christmas decorations after her mother died and never brought them out again. The one who'd worked through every holiday, leaving teenage Tessa to microwave frozen dinners alone.

"Since when do you care about Christmas festivals?" she asked before she could stop herself.

Her father's expression closed off. "People change, Tessa. At least, some of us do."

The rebuke landed exactly as intended. She'd

left Sweet River Falls and barely looked back. He'd stayed and apparently built a life that included community events, Christmas festivals, and a friendship with an ex-con who now knew him better than his own daughter did.

"I should check your blood pressure. And we need to review your medications," she said, retreating to the safety of medical procedure.

Beckett stood and began to clear the plates. "Already done this morning. Numbers were good. 128 over 82."

"I'd still like to check myself," she insisted.

Her father pushed back from the table. "Later. I need to rest now." He reached for his cane, using it to lever himself to his feet. "Beckett, we still on for that card game this afternoon?"

"Whenever you're ready," Beckett replied. "I'll finish up here first."

Her father nodded and moved toward the hallway, his gait slightly unsteady but determined. He paused at the threshold, not quite looking back at her. "Your room's yours for as long as you need it. But don't feel like you have to stay the full two weeks on my account."

He disappeared down the hall before she could respond, leaving her alone with Beckett and the dirty breakfast dishes.

"He doesn't mean it like that. He's just not good

at saying he's glad you're here," Beckett said quietly, filling the sink with soapy water.

"You don't know what he means," she replied, more sharply than she intended. "You've known him for what, six months? I'm his daughter."

He didn't react to her tone. He simply nodded, focusing on washing a plate. "You're right. I don't know your history." He glanced up, meeting her eyes briefly. "But I know he kept your room exactly as you left it. And I know he's got a photo of you in his wallet. The one from your nursing school graduation."

The revelation caught her off guard. Her father had come to her graduation and sat stiffly in the audience. He'd given her a card with a check inside, and his only comment had been that nursing was a practical choice. She hadn't known he'd kept her photo.

"The whole town will know you're back by lunchtime," he continued, changing the subject. "Small-town telegraph is faster than the internet."

"I'm not staying long enough for it to matter. Just until he's stable."

He nodded, accepting this without comment. "There's a spare key on the hook by the door if you need to go out. Grocery store's still in the same place. Pharmacy too." He paused. "Your dad usually naps in the afternoon. That might be a good time if you want to check his medications or ask more questions. He's less prickly after he rests."

The practical advice, delivered without judgment, made it hard to maintain her defensive posture. "Thank you," she said stiffly. "For helping him. And for calling 911."

"Anyone would have done the same." He rinsed the last plate and set it in the drying rack. "I'm going to chop some wood before the next snow comes in. Let me know if you need anything."

He dried his hands on a dish towel and headed for the back door, leaving her alone in the kitchen that was both achingly familiar and strangely different.

Outside the window, snow had begun to fall again, with light flakes drifting down from a pearl-gray sky. Sweet River Falls looked like a scene from a snow globe. Perfect and peaceful and completely at odds with the turmoil inside her.

She'd come prepared to manage a medical crisis and be a nurse to her estranged father. She hadn't prepared for Christmas festivals, or community expectations, or the unsettling presence of Beckett, who seemed to have carved out a place in her father's life that she'd never managed to fill.

The sound of an axe splitting wood came from the backyard in a steady rhythm, which somehow made the house feel even quieter. Two weeks suddenly stretched before her like an eternity, filled with awkward meals, town events, and the constant reminder that she was an outsider in what had once been her home.

She reached for her phone, briefly considering calling the hospital to see if they needed her back sooner. But something stopped her. Perhaps it was the memory of her supervisor's concerned face, or the panic attack that had sent her hiding in the supply closet. Or maybe it was the photo Beckett had mentioned, the one her father apparently carried in his wallet all these years.

Outside, the snow continued to fall, covering Sweet River Falls in a clean white blanket that hid all the complications beneath.

CHAPTER 3

TESSA STOOD at the sink in her father's kitchen, her fingers absently tracing the chip in the countertop that had been there since she was twelve. Nothing much had changed in this house, and yet everything felt different. The walls were the same faded yellow her mother had chosen two decades ago, but there were small touches that weren't her father's, like a well-used cookbook on the counter and a handmade wooden spoon rest by the stove.

Beckett's touches.

She glanced out the window at the snow-covered yard. The mountains rose in the distance, familiar and imposing all at once. She'd forgotten how the light hit differently here and how the air felt sharper in her lungs. Denver's city skyline suddenly seemed a world away.

She stood alone with her thoughts and a house

full of memories she'd spent years trying to outrun. The silence pressed in around her.

"I need some air." She said it out loud even though she was alone. Decision made, she grabbed her coat from the hook by the door. She hesitated, wondering if she should tell her father she was leaving, but the thought of another stilted conversation made her chest tighten. Instead, she scribbled a quick note and left it on the kitchen table.

Outside, the December cold bit at her cheeks. The path from the house to the sidewalk had been meticulously shoveled, another one of Beckett's tasks, she supposed. She saw no sign of him except for a neat stack of firewood. She tugged her scarf tighter around her neck and headed toward Main Street.

Sweet River Falls had always been picturesque, but the approaching holiday had transformed it into something straight off the front of an old-fashioned Christmas card. Garlands draped between lampposts, and storefronts twinkled with white lights. A group of volunteers was setting up what looked like a stage in the town square, likely for one of the many Christmas festivals the town had each holiday season.

She kept her head down as she passed a few familiar faces, not ready for the inevitable questions about her father or why she'd stayed away so long. But as she approached Bookish Cafe, she decided to go inside. After her mom had died, Annie, the owner, had taken Tessa under her wing. She'd tried to make things easier for a young girl who had just lost her mother. Not that it had really been possible, but Annie had been there for her. She'd heard Annie had expanded the cafe recently. As she pushed open the door, the scent of coffee and cinnamon greeted her like a welcoming committee.

"Tessa Grant, is that really you?"

Annie stood behind the counter, her hair pulled back in a complicated braid, her blue eyes wide with surprise and delight. She hurried around the counter and enveloped Tessa in a hug before she could prepare herself for the contact.

"Annie, hi," she said, awkwardly patting her back. "It's been a while."

"A while? Try a decade. I heard you were coming back because of your dad, but seeing you in the flesh is something else. You look great."

She managed a small smile. "You too. The place looks amazing."

And it did. The Bookish Cafe had expanded since she'd last been there. Bookshelves lined the walls, and a cozy reading nook with overstuffed chairs occupied one corner. A staircase led to what appeared to be a loft area, and the counter was now twice as long, displaying an array of pastries under glass domes.

"Thanks. It's been a labor of love." Annie

motioned toward a table by the window. "Sit. I'm making you a latte, and I won't take no for an answer."

Too tired to argue, she slid into the chair, grateful for the warmth of the cafe after her walk. Through the window, she could see the mountains that had been the backdrop of her childhood. She'd forgotten how they dominated everything in Sweet River Falls and how they made problems seem both insignificant and insurmountable all at once.

Annie appeared a few minutes later with two mugs and a plate of scones. "Special blend latte, just for you." She slid one of the mugs toward Tessa. "And cranberry orange scones. Fresh out of the oven."

"You didn't have to do all this."

"Please. I've been waiting years to catch up with you." Annie settled into the chair across from her. "So, ER nurse in Denver. That's impressive."

"It's just a job," she said automatically, though it had been far more than that. It had been her identity, her purpose, and her escape. Now, with her forced leave, she wasn't sure what she was anymore.

"That's not what I hear. Nora says you're some kind of medical superhero."

Tessa took a sip of her latte to avoid responding. The flavor was rich and complex, with notes of cinnamon and something else, but she had no clue what. "This is incredible."

"Secret recipe." Annie winked. "So, how long are you staying?"

"Two weeks, maybe less if Dad kicks me out first." The words came out more bitter than she'd intended.

Annie's expression softened. "He's glad you're here, even if he doesn't know how to show it."

"Right. That's why he never bothered to tell me he had an ex-con living in our house." She broke off a piece of scone, not meeting Annie's eyes.

There was a pause, and she looked up to find Annie studying her with a thoughtful expression. "Beckett's a good man. The whole town has sort of adopted him since he came here through the re-entry program."

"The whole town knows about this program?"

"Small town, remember? But it's more than that. He's earned people's trust. He fixed the roof of the church when it started leaking last spring. Helped Harrison build that new deck at Nora's cabin. He even teaches woodworking classes at the community center sometimes."

She frowned. "And no one's concerned about his past? About what he did?"

Annie took a sip of her own drink before answering. "We all know he served time. But we also know he's not defined by the worst thing that ever happened to him. None of us are."

The gentleness in Annie's voice made her throat

tighten unexpectedly. She looked away, focusing on the snow falling outside the window.

"I'm not judging him," she said, though part of her knew that wasn't entirely true. "I just... I don't understand why my father would let a stranger into our home without telling me."

"Maybe he didn't know how to tell you. You two haven't exactly been on speaking terms."

She couldn't argue with that. Their phone calls over the years had been brief and infrequent, more obligation than connection.

"And Beckett's not a stranger to your dad anymore," Annie continued. "They've been living together for six months. Stan's been doing better with him around. More social. He even came to the Harvest Festival in October."

The image of her stoic, withdrawn father at a town festival was almost impossible to reconcile with the man she knew. The man who had retreated into silence and rigid routine after her mother died and who seemed more comfortable with her academic achievements than with Tessa herself.

"I don't know who my father is anymore," she admitted quietly.

Annie reached across the table and squeezed her hand. "Maybe that's not such a bad thing. People change. Sometimes for the better."

Before she could respond, the door opened, and a gust of cold air swept into the cafe. She turned to see Beckett standing in the doorway, snowflakes clinging to his jacket and hair. His eyes found hers immediately, and something in his expression shifted—surprise, then what might have been concern.

"Sorry to interrupt," he said, his voice low. "Your father was worried when he woke up and you weren't there."

Guilt poked at her, quickly followed by annoyance. "I left a note."

"He found it. But he wanted to make sure you were okay."

Considering her father hadn't checked on her when she was a young girl, it seemed strange he'd choose now to worry about her. She was a grown woman, for Pete's sake. "You could have just called me."

"I tried. I heard your phone ringing in your room."

Now that surprised her. She never went anywhere without her phone. She felt her pockets. Nope, no phone. "Oh, sorry." Then she frowned. "Wait, you left him alone? After a stroke?" The nurse in her immediately took over, concern and professional judgment flooding her system.

He didn't flinch at her sharp tone. He simply stood there, shoulders relaxed, his gaze steady. "He's not in any immediate danger," he said calmly. "I never leave him for long. Only when he's settled in the front room with everything he needs within reach."

"But what if something happens?" she pressed, aware of Annie watching their exchange.

"I make sure his phone is charged and within reach. The neighbors check in, and I'm never gone more than thirty minutes. It's important to him to still feel some independence." His voice remained even, not defensive but matter-of-fact.

She crossed her arms. "Independence isn't worth the risk."

"With all due respect, your father disagrees. And his doctor says limited periods alone are fine at this stage." He glanced out the window at the softly falling snow. "Besides, someone needs to buy groceries and run errands. He's not up to that right now."

His words made practical sense, but it still bothered her. How could this man. who'd known her father for only six months, presume to know what was best for him?

"I'm here now. I can handle the errands."

Something flickered across his face. Not annoyance, but something closer to understanding. "That would be helpful. You could pick up his prescription at the drugstore. It's ready."

"I'll head there now." She rose from her chair.

"Then I'll head back home." He nodded at Annie and headed out the door.

Home. He called her father's cabin home.

Annie rose and collected the dishes. "Don't be a stranger while you're here, okay? We still have a lot of catching up to do."

She nodded, suddenly overwhelmed by the genuine warmth in Annie's voice. It had been a long time since anyone had looked at her with such open affection, without the expectation of competence and control that defined her life in Denver.

"Thanks for the coffee and the conversation."

She paused as she stepped outside and saw Beckett standing just outside the doorway. He was chatting with Miss Judy, the cook from Nora's lodge.

"Tessa, hi. Welcome home," Miss Judy greeted her cheerfully.

"Hey, Miss Judy. Good to see you." She smiled and headed toward the drugstore, but not before she heard Beckett and Miss Judy talking about the holiday meal drive that he was evidently helping with.

She paused at the corner, watching as Miss Judy laughed at something Beckett said. The older woman patted his arm with the easy familiarity of someone who'd known him for years, not months. It bothered her more than it should, seeing how seamlessly he'd woven himself into the community of Sweet River Falls. Into her father's life. Into her childhood home.

He belonged here in a way she no longer did.

Everyone seemed to know him, trust him, like him. The ex-con who'd somehow charmed the entire town, including her emotionally distant father. It didn't make sense. Nothing about this homecoming made sense. Not the way her father had welcomed a stranger but barely acknowledged his own daughter. Not the way the town had embraced Beckett without question.

Then a thought startled her.

She was jealous. Jealous of Beckett. Jealous of the way he fit in and she didn't. Never had really. Well, not since her mother died.

But as she continued to walk along the sidewalk in the brilliant sunshine, surrounded by clear mountain air, she started to relax. She found herself thinking about what Annie had said. *Not everyone is the sum of their worst moment.* She wondered if that applied to her too, to the ways she'd failed or the bridges she'd burned. To the panic attacks she'd been hiding from everyone at work, the trembling hands she'd been disguising, and the exhaustion that had finally caught up with her.

Maybe coming back to Sweet River Falls wasn't just about taking care of her father. Maybe, whether she wanted to admit it or not, it was about finding a way to breathe again.

TESSA CHECKED her father's vitals for the third time that morning. His blood pressure had stabilized, and his color looked better than it had the previous day. She scribbled the numbers in the small notebook she'd started keeping on the kitchen counter.

"You don't need to hover," Stan muttered, not looking up from his newspaper. "I'm not one of your patients."

"Actually, you are. That's why I'm here, remember?"

Stan folded his newspaper with a sharp crinkle. "I remember Fran overreacting and dragging you back here unnecessarily. I had a mild episode. The doctor already cleared me."

"With instructions to rest and modify your diet. And the medication schedule needs to be followed exactly."

Her father waved a dismissive hand. "Beckett's been helping with all that."

Of course, he had. Beckett, the stranger who somehow knew more about her father's medical routine than she did. Beckett, who seemed to have earned her father's trust in mere months when she'd spent decades trying.

She busied herself washing the breakfast dishes, scrubbing harder than necessary. The past few days had fallen into an uncomfortable pattern. She'd wake early, check on her father, make breakfast that he barely touched, and then spend the day trying to be useful while feeling entirely superfluous.

The sound of boots stomping snow from the porch caught her attention. A moment later, Beckett came through the door, his cheeks reddened from the cold. He carried a small stack of mail and a paper bag.

"Morning. Mail came early. And Miss Judy sent over some of those biscuits you like, Stan."

Her father's face brightened. "The cheddar ones?"

Beckett nodded, setting the bag on the table. She watched her father reach eagerly for the food, when he'd barely touched the eggs she'd made an hour ago.

Beckett hung his coat on the hook by the door. "There's a message from Annie. Something about a delivery problem at the cafe. She asked if I could stop by to help."

"The Christmas baskets," Stan said, nodding knowingly. "Every year Annie organizes food baskets for families that need extra help during the holidays. The whole town pitches in."

She vaguely remembered her mother participating in something similar years ago. Before she got sick. Before everything changed.

"I told her I'd come after lunch. Sounds like they're short on supplies and volunteers."

Stan turned to Tessa. "You should go too."

She nearly dropped the plate she was drying. "Me?"

"You've been cooped up in this house for days, and they need the help."

"I'm here to take care of you," she reminded him.

Stan snorted. "I don't need a babysitter. Go make yourself useful somewhere else for a few hours."

The familiar sting of her father's dismissal stung. Some things never changed. "Fine," she said, setting the dish towel down with forced casualness. "I'll go."

Beckett looked between them, his expression unreadable. "I'll be heading over around one if you want a ride."

"I can drive myself," she replied automatically.

"Save the gas," her father cut in. "No sense taking two vehicles to the same place."

She pressed her lips together to keep from arguing. "One o'clock, then."

Beckett nodded once and headed toward the basement stairs, where he'd been working on some project. The door closed behind him with a soft click.

Left alone with her father again, she felt the unspoken words hanging between them. Had he always been this difficult, or had she simply forgotten? Or maybe she was the difficult one, still nursing old wounds that everyone else had moved past.

"I'm going to take a shower." She needed to escape the suffocating silence. Her father merely grunted in acknowledgment, already reabsorbed in his newspaper.

Under the hot spray of water, she tried to quiet her thoughts. She'd come here with one clear purpose. She needed to tend to her father's medical needs, ensure his recovery was on track, and then return to Denver.

Simple. Clinical. Manageable.

Except nothing about being back in Sweet River Falls felt manageable. Every interaction with her father reopened old hurts. Every glimpse of Beckett's easy rapport with him was salt in those wounds. And now she was being volunteered for community service she hadn't planned for.

The water began to cool, forcing her to finish her shower. As she toweled off, she caught her reflection in the mirror. There were dark circles under her eyes, and her skin looked pale. She hadn't been sleeping well, torn between hypervigilance over her father's condition and unsettling dreams about the hospital.

The memory of her hands shaking as she tried to place an IV made her stomach clench. She'd hidden in the supply closet, gasping for air, convinced she was having a heart attack until Dr. Foster had found her and recognized the panic attack for what it was.

"Take some time," he'd told her. "Get help. This job will eat you alive if you let it."

She hadn't told anyone here about her leave of absence. Not even her father knew she was on highly suggested medical leave rather than vacation. It was easier that way. Simpler to be the competent caregiver than admit she was barely holding herself together.

By the time one o'clock rolled around, she had changed clothes twice, unsure what to wear for community service in a town she barely recognized anymore. She settled on jeans and a flannel shirt, practical enough for whatever tasks awaited.

Beckett was already waiting by his truck when she stepped onto the porch. The vehicle was older but well-maintained, much like the man himself.

"Your chariot," he said with the barest hint of a smile, opening the passenger door.

The ride to town was quiet but not entirely uncomfortable. He seemed content with silence, focusing on navigating the snowy roads with careful attention. She found herself studying his profile when he wasn't looking. There was a steadiness to him that she hadn't noticed before, a calm centeredness that contrasted sharply with her own internal chaos.

"Your father's doing better," he said eventually, breaking the silence. "His speech is clearer every day."

She nodded. "The medication is helping. But he needs to be more careful with his diet."

"He's stubborn."

A surprised laugh escaped her. "That's putting it mildly."

"He reminds me of my grandfather. The man would argue with a fence post if he thought it was in his way."

The small moment of shared understanding faded as they pulled up behind Bookish Cafe. The back door stood propped open despite the cold, and people were carrying boxes in and out.

Annie spotted them immediately, waving them over with visible relief. Her hair was pulled back in a messy braid, and she wore a Christmas sweater adorned with tiny bells that jingled as she moved.

"Thank goodness," she said. "We've got a situation."

Beckett stepped forward. "What happened?"

"The delivery truck that was supposed to bring most of our canned goods got diverted to Grand Junction. We're short about half of what we need, and the baskets go out tomorrow morning."

The back room of the cafe had been transformed into a makeshift assembly line. Tables were covered with food items, empty baskets waited to be filled, and volunteers moved between stations helping where they could.

"Nora's at the lodge gathering whatever they can spare from their pantry. And I've called everyone I can think of for donations, but we're still going to be short."

"What do you need us to do?" Tessa surprised herself with her eagerness to help.

Annie looked relieved. "Beckett, can you take over the assembly station? And Tessa, I could use help sorting what we do have and figuring out how to stretch it."

They separated to their assigned tasks, and Tessa found herself at a table covered with canned vegetables, pasta, and various dry goods. A woman with silver-streaked hair was already there, making notes on a clipboard.

"You must be Stan's daughter," the woman said,

extending her hand. "I'm Lucy. My husband and I run Pine View B&B."

"Nice to meet you." She shook Lucy's hand.

"We've heard a lot about you from your father. He's very proud of your nursing career."

She blinked in surprise. Her father, proud? That didn't align with anything she knew about Stan Grant.

"We need to count everything and divide it evenly among forty baskets," Lucy explained, seemingly unaware of Tessa's confusion. "Each basket should have enough for several meals."

She nodded, grateful for the task. Numbers and inventory were straightforward, uncomplicated by emotional undercurrents. She began counting and sorting, quickly falling into a rhythm.

From her position, she could see Beckett directing volunteers at the assembly station. He worked with quiet efficiency, his instructions clear and his movements purposeful. People responded to him without hesitation, following his lead as if he'd been organizing this event for years.

"He's been such a blessing to this town," Lucy commented, following Tessa's gaze. "Fixed the library roof, built new shelves for the school, and teaches those woodworking classes at the community center."

"I heard." She turned back to her counting.

Lucy smiled. "Your father speaks very highly of

him. Says he's never met anyone who works harder or complains less."

The comment stung more than it should have. When had her father ever spoken highly of her to others? Even her decision to become a nurse had been met with practical approval rather than pride.

"We're short on protein," she noted, changing the subject. "Not enough canned meat or beans."

Lucy sighed. "That's what I was afraid of. The protein items were on the missing delivery."

"What about peanut butter? It's shelf-stable and high in protein," she suggested.

"Good thinking. I'll check with Annie."

As Lucy walked away, Tessa continued organizing the available food. The work was methodical and soothing, allowing her mind to focus on something besides her father's condition and her own uncertain future.

Eventually, her sorting system brought her to the assembly station where Beckett was working. They found themselves side by side, packing boxes with carefully measured portions of food.

"You're good at this," he observed after watching her efficient movements.

She shrugged. "I'm used to organizing medical supplies. This isn't so different."

He placed a bag of rice in a basket. "Your father mentioned you work in an emergency room. That must be challenging."

"It has its moments." She was unwilling to discuss how challenging it had recently become and how the job she'd once found purpose in now filled her with dread.

They worked in silence for a while, finding an unexpected rhythm together. He would open a new box, she would arrange the base items, and he would add the heavier cans. It was oddly comfortable, this wordless cooperation.

"How long have you been away from Sweet River Falls?" he eventually asked.

"Ten, maybe fifteen years. I left for nursing school and never really came back except for brief visits."

"It's a good town. People here look out for each other."

"So I've noticed," she said, thinking of how quickly he'd been accepted. How easily he'd slipped into a place in her father's life.

"Your father talks about you. Keeps a photo of you on his nightstand."

She paused, a can of corn suspended in her hand. "He does?"

He nodded. "Told me you were the smartest person in your class. Said you always knew you wanted to help people."

Something tightened in her chest. "We don't talk much."

"I gathered that. But he notices when you send cards. Keeps them in his dresser drawer."

The revelation left her momentarily speechless. She'd sent those cards out of obligation, brief notes for birthdays and holidays. She'd never imagined her father saving them, much less showing them to anyone else.

"Stan's not great at saying what he feels," he continued, carefully placing a small bag of flour in a basket. "But that doesn't mean he doesn't feel it."

She wasn't sure how to respond. This stranger seemed to understand her father in ways she never had, or perhaps had never tried to.

"Why are you telling me this?" she finally asked.

"Because everyone deserves a second chance. Even fathers and daughters."

Before she could reply, Annie called out from across the room.

"We've got more supplies coming in! Nora worked a miracle at the lodge."

The moment broken, she returned her attention to the baskets. But Beckett's words lingered, stirring up questions she'd long ago stopped asking.

The afternoon passed in a blur of activity. More volunteers arrived with donations, tables were rearranged to accommodate the new supplies, and the assembly line grew more efficient. Beckett came over and said Stan had checked in twice and was doing fine. By four o'clock, they had completed most of the baskets.

"We'll finish the rest tomorrow morning," Annie announced to the tired volunteers. "You've all been amazing. Thank you."

People began dispersing, gathering coats, and saying goodbyes. She found herself helping with cleanup, wiping down tables, and organizing left-over supplies.

Beckett approached as she was folding the last empty box. "Ready to head back?"

She nodded, suddenly aware of how tired she felt. The physical work had been a welcome distrac-tion, but now exhaustion was settling into her bones.

As they walked to his truck, snow began falling in large, lazy flakes. The street lamps were coming on, painting a warm glow over the darkening town. Christmas lights twinkled from storefronts and lampposts, transforming Main Street into something magical.

"It's pretty here," she admitted, tilting her face up to feel the snowflakes on her skin. "I forgot how beautiful winter can be in the mountains."

He watched her for a moment, something unreadable in his expression. "Some things are worth coming back for."

The drive home was quiet again, but the silence felt different. Less tense. Almost comfortable. As they pulled into the driveway, she noticed the porch light was on and smoke curled from the chimney. Her father must have started a fire in the old wood stove.

"Thank you," she said before getting out of the truck. "For the ride. And for what you said about my father."

He nodded. "Just telling the truth."

Inside, they found Stan dozing in his recliner, the television playing softly in the background. A pot of something that smelled like beef stew simmered on the stove.

"You cooked?" she asked in surprise when her father stirred awake.

"Heated up," Stan corrected. "Miss Judy sent it over with Jason this afternoon. Said you two would be hungry after helping with the baskets."

The thoughtfulness of the gesture caught her off guard. "That was nice of her."

"This town takes care of its own," Stan said, pushing himself up from the chair. "Always has."

As they settled around the kitchen table with bowls of steaming stew, she found herself wondering if she still counted as one of Sweet River Falls's own. And even more surprisingly, whether she might want to.

CHAPTER 5

Tessa ran her fingers along the built-in bookshelf that lined one wall of her father's living room. The house felt stuffy after three days of being cooped up inside. The snow had fallen steadily since her arrival, keeping them mostly housebound except for their brief outing to help with the Christmas baskets.

Her father dozed in his recliner, a thin afghan covering his legs. The television played some home renovation show with the volume turned low. Beckett had gone out to shovel the driveway again, insisting that Stan shouldn't worry about the accumulation.

She scanned the shelves, noting the familiar books from her childhood. Her mother's collection of poetry anthologies remained untouched, gathering dust in the corner. A row of photo albums caught her eye, leather-bound volumes she hadn't seen in years.

Curious, she pulled one from the shelf. The cover was worn at the edges, and the once-bright red had faded to a dull burgundy. She carried it to the couch and curled up in the corner, tucking her feet beneath her.

The first page held formal portraits of people she barely recognized from her father's side of the family. She flipped forward, pausing when she reached photos from her parents' wedding. Her mother looked radiant in a simple white dress, her dark hair falling in waves around her shoulders. Her father stood tall beside her, looking impossibly young and... happy. His smile stretched wide across his face, his arm wrapped firmly around his new bride's waist.

She swallowed hard. She couldn't remember the last time she'd seen her father smile like that.

She turned the pages slowly, watching as the formal portraits gave way to candid snapshots. Her parents on a camping trip. Her mother pregnant, her hand resting on her rounded belly. And then, baby pictures. Tessa as a newborn, swaddled in a yellow blanket. Her father holding her, looking terrified and proud all at once.

A photo slipped from between the pages and fluttered to the floor. Tessa leaned down to pick it up, her breath catching when she saw the image.

She couldn't have been more than four or five, sitting on her mother's lap at the kitchen table. They were making cookies, both of their hands covered in flour, both laughing at whoever was behind the camera—her father, presumably.

She slid the photo back into place and continued turning pages. The images documented birthday parties, first days of school, and family vacations. Then, abruptly, the photos changed. Her mother disappeared from the frames. Tessa grew older, her smile dimming. The pictures became more formal and less frequent. School portraits. Awards ceremonies. Her high school graduation.

The last few pages held newspaper clippings of her nursing school graduation and a photo someone had taken of her in her scrubs during her first week at Denver Memorial. She hadn't known her father had kept track of these milestones.

"Found the old albums, huh?"

She startled, looking up to find her father awake and watching her. "Yeah. I was just... reminiscing, I guess."

Stan nodded, adjusting himself in the recliner. "Your mother was the one who kept those up to date. I tried to add to them after... well, after. But I was never good at remembering to take pictures."

"I remember she always had a camera with her," Tessa said softly.

"Said you never knew when a moment worth

capturing would happen." He cleared his throat. "She was right about that."

She closed the album, her fingers lingering on the cover. "I miss her."

"Yeah." He looked away, his jaw tightening. "Me too."

The front door opened, bringing a gust of cold air and Beckett, his shoulders dusted with snow and his cheeks ruddy from exertion.

"It's really coming down out there. Driveway's clear for now, but we might need to do it again before dinner."

"Thanks, Beckett," Stan said. "Appreciate it."

She watched the easy exchange between the two men, and that familiar twinge of jealousy returned. She stood, tucking the album under her arm. "I think I'll make some tea. Anyone else want some?"

Stan shook his head, but Beckett nodded. "That sounds great. Let me just get out of these wet things."

In the kitchen, she filled the kettle and set it on the stove. She placed the photo album on the counter, unable to resist opening it again to the picture of her and her mother baking. The memory was hazy, but she could almost smell the spices and feel the warmth of her mother's arms around her as they mixed the dough.

On impulse, she moved to the wooden recipe box that sat on a shelf above the microwave. It had been her mother's, a wedding gift from a great-aunt. She lifted the lid and found the box still full of recipe cards in her mother's neat handwriting.

She flipped through them, pausing when she found one labeled "Ginger Molasses Cookies (Gravy Cookies) Tessa's Favorite." Gravy cookies. How long had it been since she'd thought of them? When she was a young girl, she had called them gravy cookies because of the icing her mom put on them. She thought the icing looked like gravy. Her mother had laughed, and from then on, they were called gravy cookies. She smiled at the memory.

She stared at the card, splattered with old ingredients, and the corners dog-eared from frequent use. She could almost smell them baking, how they filled the house with the smell of ginger and molasses, and how her mother would let her lick the spoon after they dropped the last cookie onto the baking sheet.

The kettle whistled, pulling her from the memory. She made two mugs of tea and handed one to Beckett when he entered the kitchen in dry clothes.

"Thanks." He wrapped his hands around the mug and nodded toward the recipe box. "Planning to do some cooking?"

"Maybe. These were my favorite when I was little. My mom used to make them every Christmas. Gravy cookies." She picked up the recipe card.

"Gravy cookies?"

"Yeah, don't ask." She shook her head.

He smiled as he leaned against the counter and blew on his tea. "Your dad mentioned those once. Said they smelled like the holidays to him."

"He did?" She looked toward the living room, where she could hear the television volume increase slightly.

"Yeah. Miss Judy made gingerbread cookies for the lodge last month, and your dad said they reminded him of something your mom used to make, but they weren't quite the same."

She studied the recipe card, noting the ingredients. Basic pantry staples, nothing fancy. "I wonder if we have everything."

"Only one way to find out. I can help if you want. Though I should warn you, I'm better at eating cookies than making them."

For the first time since arriving in Sweet River Falls, she felt a genuine smile form. "Let me check the pantry."

To her surprise, they had almost everything they needed. She found flour and sugar. The spices were there, though the ginger was nearly empty. The only thing missing was molasses.

"I could run out and get some," Beckett offered.

She hesitated, looking at the snow still falling outside the window. "I don't want you to have to go back out in this."

"It's no problem. I need to pick up a few things for dinner anyway. Any other requests while I'm there?" He finished his tea and set the mug in the sink.

"I guess get more ginger and the molasses. Thank you." She handed him some cash from her wallet, which he tried to refuse.

"I've got it covered. Save that for something else."

"Please, take it. I'm the one who wants to make the cookies."

He relented, tucking the money into his pocket. "I'll be back in a bit."

After he left, she gathered the rest of the ingredients and began measuring them out. She found her mother's old mixing bowls in a lower cabinet, still in the same place after all these years. The familiar weight of the ceramic bowl in her hands brought back more memories.

Her father appeared in the doorway, leaning on his cane. "What are you up to in here?"

She held up the recipe card. "I found Mom's recipe for gravy cookies. Thought I might make a batch."

Something flickered across his face, too quick for her to identify. "Haven't had those in a long time."

"Not since Mom died," she said quietly.

He nodded, his gaze dropping to the floor. "Need any help?"

The offer surprised her. "Um, sure. Beckett went to get molasses, but we could start creaming the butter and sugar."

He shuffled to the table and lowered himself into a chair. "I'll supervise from here, if that's all right. Doctor said I should take it easy."

"That's fine." She brought the butter and sugar to the table, along with the mixing bowl and a wooden spoon. She sat across from her father and began working the butter with the spoon to soften it.

"Your mother always used to let the butter sit out overnight. Said it made for better cookies."

"I remember." She added the sugar and continued mixing. "But I'm impatient."

Stan's lips rose in what might have been a smile. "You get that from me. Your mother was the patient one."

They sat in companionable silence as she worked, the only sound the scrape of the spoon against the bowl. It was the longest they'd been alone together without tension since she'd arrived.

"I miss these cookies," she admitted. "I tried making them once in my apartment, but they didn't taste the same."

"Probably the altitude," he offered. "Your mom always said that baking's different up here in the mountains."

"Maybe." Or maybe it was because her mother

wasn't there, guiding her hands and laughing when she spilled flour on the floor.

The front door opened, and Beckett came inside, holding a grocery bag. "Got the molasses and a few other things."

He entered the kitchen, setting the bag on the counter. "They were almost out of molasses. Apparently, everyone's baking this week."

She rose to retrieve the bottle. "Thanks for going. We've got the butter and sugar ready."

"Don't let me interrupt. I'll just unpack these things and put them away, then I've got some work to do in the shed."

"You don't have to go back out in the cold. You could help us with the cookies."

Beckett glanced at Stan, who nodded almost imperceptibly. "Well, if you're sure I won't be in the way."

"Not at all. Mom always said baking was better with company."

The three of them worked together, with Tessa mixing, Beckett helping measure ingredients, and Stan offering occasional comments about how her mother used to do things. By the time the dough was ready, the kitchen was warm and fragrant with spices.

"The recipe says to chill the dough for an hour or overnight." She frowned.

"Your mother rarely bothered with that. She'd just bake them right away."

"But it says right here——"

"I know what it says," Stan interrupted, but his tone was gentle. "But she always claimed she didn't have time to wait when she had a hungry husband and daughter."

"Okay, then we'll bake them now since I have two hungry men in the kitchen."

She preheated the oven and prepared two baking sheets. She and Beckett took turns rolling the dough into balls, then flattening them, while Stan watched from his seat at the table.

"These look right," Stan said as she slid the first batch into the oven. "Your mother would approve."

The compliment, small as it was, warmed her more than she expected. "Thanks, Dad."

As the cookies baked, the kitchen filled with the rich, spicy aroma of ginger and molasses. She closed her eyes, inhaling deeply. For a moment, she could almost believe she was eight years old again, waiting impatiently for the timer to ding so she could have the first warm cookie.

When she opened her eyes, she caught her father wiping quickly at his face.

"Dad? Are you okay?"

He nodded, not meeting her gaze. "Just the spices. They make my eyes water."

Beckett tactfully busied himself with washing the mixing bowls, giving them a moment of privacy.

"They smell just like Mom's," she said softly.

Stan cleared his throat. "Yeah. They do."

She made up a batch of the icing while the cookies baked. The timer dinged, and she retrieved the first batch from the oven. The cookies were perfect, with golden edges. She let them cool for a few minutes before transferring them to a wire rack. She drizzled the icing on each cookie.

Beckett walked over and looked over her shoulder. "Hey, I can see how a kid would think that icing looks a bit like gravy." He grinned at her.

She smiled at him, then turned and offered one to her father. "Here, first one's for you."

He took the cookie, and his hand trembled slightly. He took a bite, closing his eyes as he chewed. When he opened them again, they were definitely misty.

"Just like hers. You did good, Tessa." His voice sounded rough.

"Thanks, Dad." She offered a cookie to Beckett, who accepted it with a grateful nod.

"These are amazing," he said after taking a bite. "Best cookies I've had in years."

She took one for herself, the warm spices filling her mouth, transporting her back to Christmas mornings and snow days and quiet evenings around the kitchen table. Her mother might be gone, but this small piece of her remained, preserved in a handwritten recipe card and the memory of flour-covered hands.

As she watched her father take another cookie, his eyes still suspiciously bright, she felt something shift between them. Not forgiveness, not yet. But perhaps understanding. And for now, that was enough.

CHAPTER 6

BECKETT'S SHOVEL cut through the fresh snow with a satisfying crunch. The early morning sun spilled across Stan's driveway as he worked, his breath clouding in the crisp air. He'd been up since five, with thoughts rambling through his mind, unable to fall back asleep. Worries about Stan's recovery—though the man was doing remarkably well—and then the tension between Stan and Tessa.

Tessa.

He paused, leaning against the shovel for a moment. Her presence in the house had shifted everything, like someone had rearranged all the furniture just enough to make him bump into things. He wasn't sure if it was a good change or not, but it was definitely a change.

Yesterday had been something. The way her

face had softened when she found that cookie recipe, and how Stan had actually volunteered to help instead of grumbling about resting. For a brief moment, the three of them had existed in the kitchen without all the tension that usually stretched between father and daughter like a tripwire.

He resumed shoveling, working methodically down the driveway. The physical labor helped him think. It always had. Prison had taught him to find clarity in routine tasks and use the repetitive motion to sort through whatever was on his mind.

And Tessa Grant was definitely on his mind.

She surprised him the other day at the Bookish Cafe. He'd expected her to hang back, maybe even refuse to come altogether. Instead, she'd thrown herself into organizing the Christmas baskets with the same focused efficiency he imagined she brought to her nursing. The way she'd quickly assessed what needed doing, then quietly taken charge of the sorting system without making anyone feel ordered around or inadequate.

He'd watched her hands while she worked, noting how steady they were when handling the donations, and how gentle they were when showing a child how to arrange items in a basket. Nurse's hands. Capable hands.

But he'd also seen how those same hands trembled slightly when she thought no one was looking.

How she'd flex her fingers and take deep breaths when she thought she was alone.

Something was off. He recognized the signs because he'd lived them himself. The careful control, the hidden moments of vulnerability, and the way she sometimes seemed to retreat inside herself even while standing in a crowded room.

Tessa Grant was hiding something. Not just from her father, but maybe from herself too.

He scooped up another shovelful of snow, tossing it onto the growing bank beside the driveway. The physical exertion felt good and felt productive. Unlike his thoughts about Tessa, which were getting him nowhere he had any business going.

It wasn't his place to wonder about her secrets. He was here to help Stan, to fulfill his obligations to the reentry program, and rebuild some semblance of a life. Getting tangled up in family drama between Stan and his daughter wasn't part of the deal.

But he couldn't help noticing things. Like the haunted look that sometimes crossed her face when she thought no one was watching. The way her smile never quite reached her eyes. The careful distance she maintained, not just from her father but from everyone.

He recognized that pain because he carried his

own version of it. The difference was, he'd earned his through his own poor choices. What was Tessa running from?

"You're out here early."

The voice startled him. He turned to find Tessa standing at the edge of the garage, bundled in a heavy coat, her hands wrapped around a steaming mug.

"Morning," he said, nodding toward her. "Didn't mean to wake you."

"You didn't. I'm usually up early." She handed him the insulated mug. "Thought you might want this."

He took the mug. "Thank you."

She stepped off the steps, her boots crunching in the snow. "You don't have to do this every day, you know. The driveway."

"I don't mind. It helps me think."

"About what?"

He considered how much truth to offer. "About yesterday. Those cookies seemed to mean a lot to your dad."

Something flickered across her face. Surprise, maybe. Or suspicion that he was trying to manipulate her with sentiment.

"Yeah. I didn't expect him to remember about the cookies, much less want to help make them."

"He talks about your mom sometimes. Not

often, but when he does, it's always with a lot of love."

Her expression turned guarded again. "He never talked about her when I was growing up. After she died, it was like she never existed."

He nodded, understanding more than he could say. "Grief does strange things to people. Makes them shut down when they should open up."

"Is that what happened to you?" The question was direct, her gaze steady on his face.

He felt the familiar tension at being asked about his past. But something about the early morning quiet and the honest curiosity in her eyes made him answer.

"Different kind of loss. But yeah, I shut down too. For a long time."

She seemed to consider this, her eyes searching his face. Whatever she was looking for, he wasn't sure she found it.

"Dad seems to trust you," she finally said.

"We understand each other." He set his coffee on the step and resumed shoveling.

"I should check on Dad," she said, abruptly changing the subject. "Make sure he takes his morning medication."

He nodded.

As she turned to go back inside, she paused. "Thanks. For being here for him when I wasn't."

Before he could respond, she was gone, the door closing softly behind her.

He stared after her, feeling like something important had just happened, though for the life of him, he couldn't quite name what it was. He returned to his shoveling, thinking that maybe the rift between Stan and Tessa wasn't the only thing beginning to thaw in the winter cold.

CHAPTER 7

TESSA EYED her father with concern as he buttoned his coat. His hands moved more slowly than she remembered, and his fingers fumbled with the buttons. She resisted the urge to step in and help, knowing it would only irritate him.

"Are you sure you're up for this, Dad? We could skip the festival if you're not feeling well." She deliberately kept her tone casual.

"Are you sure you're up for this, Dad? We could skip the festival if you're not feeling well." She deliberately kept her tone casual.

Stan shot her a look that hadn't changed in fifteen years. "I'm fine. I'm judging the gingerbread contest. Can't let everyone down. Been judging for half a dozen years now."

Beckett appeared from the hallway, dressed in a flannel shirt and his worn work jacket. His eyes met hers briefly before he reached for his boots. "Lodge will be packed tonight. Miss Judy's been baking for days."

"She still makes those cinnamon rolls?" she asked, memories of childhood breakfasts at the lodge surfacing unexpectedly.

"Best in Colorado. She sets some aside for Stan every first and third Sunday of the month."

Another revelation that caught Tessa off guard. Her father had Sunday rituals with the lodge cook? The same father who used to scoff at community gatherings?

The drive to Sweet River Lodge was short but beautiful. Fresh snow blanketed the pines, and Christmas lights twinkled along the fences of properties they passed. Tessa sat in the back seat of her father's truck, watching as Beckett and Stan exchanged comfortable conversation about the weather and local gossip. The easy rapport between them still unsettled her.

Sweet River Lodge came into view, its windows glowing with warm light against the darkening sky. Cars filled the parking area, and she could see figures moving about inside the main building. Smoke curled from the stone chimney, and Christmas music drifted through the air. "Looks like the whole town showed up."

"Always do," Stan said as Beckett pulled into a space marked 'Reserved for Judge Grant' with a handwritten sign.

She couldn't help but smile at the small-town

charm of it all. In Denver, she'd been too busy working double shifts to notice Christmas approaching. Here, it was impossible to ignore.

The main lodge was transformed. Garlands of pine and twinkling lights hung from the rafters. A massive stone fireplace crackled with flames at one end of the room, surrounded by comfortable seating. Tables lined the walls, laden with cookies, hot chocolate, and mulled cider. At the center of it all stood a display of gingerbread houses, each more elaborate than the last.

"Stan!" Nora Cassidy hurried over, her gray-streaked hair pulled back in a neat bun. She wore a festive red sweater with a small Christmas tree pin. "And Beckett! So glad you made it." Her warm eyes settled on Tessa. "And Tessa Grant. Welcome home, dear."

"Thank you," she said, surprised by the genuine warmth in Nora's greeting. "The lodge looks beautiful."

"We go all out for Christmas," Nora beamed. "Stan, the other judges are waiting by the gingerbread display. Beckett, would you mind helping Jason hang the last of the lights outside before the tree lighting? And Tessa, come with me. Annie's been asking about you."

Before she could respond, Nora had linked arms with her and was guiding her through the crowd.

People nodded and smiled as they passed. Some called out greetings, using her name with easy familiarity.

"Tessa! Good to see you back!"

"How long are you staying, Tessa?"

"Merry Christmas, Tessa!"

She smiled and nodded, feeling oddly seen in a way she hadn't in years. In Denver, she was just another nurse, another face in scrubs rushing through hospital corridors. Here, she was Tessa Grant, the prodigal daughter returning at last, even if it was only temporarily.

Annie waved from behind a table where she was serving hot chocolate. She wore a blue sweater with snowflakes.

"There you are!" Annie exclaimed. "I saved you some of the good hot chocolate. The kind with real melted chocolate, not the powdered stuff."

She accepted the steaming mug. "Thanks. I can't believe how many people are here."

"Sweet River Falls does love a good festival. And Nora throws the best ones. How's your dad doing?"

"Better than I expected, actually. Though he's pushing himself too hard."

Annie nodded knowingly. "Stan's always been stubborn. But he's changed a lot these past few years. Opened up more since Beckett came along."

"So I've noticed. Everyone keeps talking about how different he is. It's... strange."

"People change, Tessa. Sometimes they just need the right reason. Your dad's been trying, in his own way."

"Has he?" The words came out more sharply than she intended.

Annie didn't flinch. "When you sent that card last Christmas, he brought it to the cafe to show me."

She stared into her mug. The card had been a last-minute thing, a generic holiday greeting with her signature. She'd sent it out of obligation, not expecting her father to treasure it.

"I should check on him," she said finally, needing space to process this new information.

She found her father at the gingerbread display, clipboard in hand, studying each creation with serious concentration. A small crowd had gathered to watch the judging, and Tessa hung back, observing.

"The structural integrity on this one is impressive," Stan was saying to the other judges, pointing to a gingerbread replica of the town's Main Street. "Look at how they reinforced the shop awnings."

The other judges nodded, making notes. Stan moved to the next display, a gingerbread version of Sweet River Lodge complete with tiny pine trees and a frozen sugar lake.

"Attention to detail here is remarkable. See how

they got the exact number of windows on the main building?" he commented.

She watched, fascinated. Her father had always been precise and detail-oriented, but she'd never seen him channel those traits into something that brought joy to others. He looked different too, more animated, and his eyes were bright with interest.

People kept approaching him, clapping him on the shoulder, asking his opinion. And he responded to each one with more words than she had heard him string together in years. This wasn't the withdrawn, emotionally distant father she'd left behind. This was a man embedded in his community, respected and valued.

After the judging concluded and ribbons were awarded, she made her way to her father's side.

"The structural integrity one, huh?" she said, nodding toward the Main Street display that had won first place.

Stan looked pleased. "Engineering always beats flash. That one would stand up to a real snowstorm."

"You seemed to be enjoying yourself."

"Been doing this a while now. Got a system." He gave a small shrug.

She noticed the slight droop to his shoulders, the way he leaned more heavily on his cane. "You look tired, Dad. Maybe we should head home."

"Not until the tree lighting. It's the best part," he said firmly.

Before she could argue, Miss Judy appeared with a plate of cookies. "Stan Grant, you did a fine job judging. Fair as always." She turned to Tessa with a warm smile. "Your father talks about you all the time, you know."

"He does?" She wondered just how many people in this town her father actually talked to about her.

"Oh yes. Always telling us about his daughter, the nurse, saving lives in Denver. Try one of these. Old family recipe." Miss Judy handed her a cookie.

The cookie was still warm, buttery, and sweet. "It's delicious," she said honestly.

"Your father brings me your mother's recipes sometimes," Miss Judy said. "Says I'm the only one who might do them justice. That's high praise from Stan."

She glanced at her father, who was suddenly very interested in his own cookie. Another piece of the puzzle shifted into place. Her father hadn't forgotten her mother. He'd been keeping her memory alive in his own quiet way.

The evening continued with carolers performing by the fireplace and children running about with paper reindeer antlers on their heads. She found herself relaxing, caught up in the festive atmosphere. She spotted Beckett across the room, helping an elderly woman to a seat near the fire. His movements were careful and considerate. When he looked up and caught her watching, she didn't look away.

At last, Nora called for everyone's attention. The crowd quieted as she stood near the lodge's front entrance.

"Friends and neighbors," she began, her voice carrying clearly through the room. "Thank you all for coming to our annual Christmas Festival. As always, your presence makes this event special. Sweet River Falls isn't just a place on a map. It's a community of people who care for each other, who show up when it matters."

Murmurs of agreement rippled through the crowd.

"Tonight, as we light our Christmas tree, I want us to remember what makes this town special. It's not just our beautiful mountains or our lovely lake. It's all of you. Every person who calls Sweet River Falls home, whether they've been here for generations or just arrived." Her gaze swept the room, lingering briefly on Tessa and Beckett. "Everyone belongs here."

The words wrapped around her like a hug. Belonged here. When was the last time she'd felt like she truly belonged anywhere?

"Now, let's head outside for the lighting of the tree!"

The crowd moved out onto the wide porch and lawn of the lodge. A massive pine tree stood near the entrance, strung with lights but still dark. She stood beside her father and Beckett, their breath forming clouds in the cold air.

"Ten!" Nora called, and the crowd joined in the countdown. "Nine! Eight!"

She glanced at her father, who was watching the tree with childlike anticipation.

"Seven! Six! Five!"

Beckett stood on her father's other side, steady and watchful as always.

"Four! Three! Two! One!"

The tree burst into light, a cascade of twinkling colors against the dark sky. The crowd cheered, and she found herself smiling. It was simple, perhaps even a bit corny, but undeniably magical.

"Beautiful," her father murmured, and she wasn't sure if he was talking to her or himself.

After the lighting, Stan finally admitted to being tired. The drive home was quiet, all three of them content in the silence. When they arrived, Beckett helped Stan up the front steps while Tessa unlocked the door.

"I'm turning in," Stan announced once inside. "Been a long day."

"Do you need help with anything?" she asked.

Her father paused, then shook his head. "I can manage. Good night, Tessa. Beckett."

"Good night, Dad."

After he'd gone to his room, she found herself reluctant to retreat to her own. Beckett started a fire with practiced ease, and its flames created a cozy atmosphere in the room.

"Want some tea?" he asked, already moving toward the kitchen.

"That would be nice."

She settled on the couch while Beckett prepared the tea. Through the window, she could see snowflakes beginning to fall again, gentle and unhurried. In Denver, snow meant traffic jams and hospital emergencies. Here, it was simply part of the rhythm of life.

He returned with two mugs, handing one to her before taking a seat in the armchair across from her. The fire crackled in the hearth, spilling a warm glow across the room.

"He did well today," Beckett said after a moment. "But he'll be tired tomorrow."

"I noticed. I'll make sure he rests." She cradled her mug, breathing in the herbal scent. "I still can't believe how involved he is in the town. The father I remember barely spoke to the neighbors."

He nodded thoughtfully. "People can surprise you. Sometimes they just need time."

"Or the right person to help them change." She met his gaze directly.

He looked away, uncomfortable with the implied

compliment. "Your father's a good man. Always has been, I think."

She considered this. "Maybe. But he wasn't always good at showing it."

"Grief does that to people. Makes them forget how to connect."

The simple truth of his words settled over her. Wasn't that what had happened to her too? After her mother died, she'd learned to be self-sufficient, expect nothing from others, and keep her emotions tightly controlled. It had made her an excellent nurse but a guarded human being.

"I'm starting to think Sweet River Falls has some kind of magic," she said, changing the subject. "Everyone seems so... connected here."

"It's a special place. Took me by surprise too."

"How did you end up here?" The question had been on her mind since she arrived.

He was quiet for a long moment, and she thought he might not answer. "The reentry program I was in partnered with communities willing to take a chance on people like me. Your father volunteered. Said he had the space and could use the help."

"That doesn't sound like my father at all."

"People change." He echoed Annie's words from earlier. "Sometimes they just need the right reason."

They fell into a comfortable silence, watching the fire. She realized she felt more relaxed than she had in months. No beeping monitors, no emergency calls, and no constant pressure of life-or-death decisions. Just the quiet of a snowy evening, the warmth of tea, and the unexpected comfort of Beckett's presence.

"I think I needed this," she said softly, more to herself than to him.

"The tea?" he asked with a hint of a smile.

"No. This." She gestured vaguely at the room, the falling snow outside, and the peaceful moment they were sharing. "Slowing down. I've been running for so long, I forgot how to stop."

He nodded, understanding in his eyes. "Sweet River Falls is good for that. Reminds you to breathe."

She took a deep breath, as if testing his theory. The air smelled of smoke from the fire and the herbal tea in her hands. They were simple, comforting ones.

"I think you're right." Something tight within her began to loosen. For the first time since arriving, she didn't feel the urgent need to check her phone for messages from the hospital or to mentally calculate how many days until she could return to Denver.

Instead, she found herself wondering what the River Walk looked like under a full blanket of fresh snow and whether they still lined the walk with Christmas lights. She wanted to try Miss Judy's cinnamon rolls and visit the bookstore section of Annie's cafe. Small curiosities, but they tugged at her with surprising strength.

As she sat there in the quiet house with the steady presence of Beckett across from her, she realized something unexpected. Part of her—a part she'd long ignored—was glad to be home.

CHAPTER 8

TESSA WOKE to the sound of a distant snowplow rumbling down the street. She lay in her childhood bed, staring at the ceiling. The memory of her mother helping her put up those glowing stars on her ceiling flashed through her mind. Her mom helped her shape them into constellations. She glanced at the window where the curtains her mother had sewn for her still hung, faded now, but still there.

For a moment, she let herself be still. No alarms blaring, no overhead announcements, no rush to check vitals or administer medication. Surrounded by comforting memories. Just peaceful quiet, punctuated only by the occasional scrape of the plow against asphalt.

She couldn't remember the last time she'd had a

morning without urgency. Enjoyed a morning without pressure.

Down the hall, she could hear her father's voice mingling with Beckett's, their words indistinct but their tones comfortable. Last night's conversation with Beckett by the fire had left her unsettled. Not because of anything he'd said, but because of how much she'd wanted to keep talking. How for the first time in years, she'd felt the tightness in her chest loosen just a little.

She pushed back the covers and padded to the window. Fresh snow blanketed the yard, pristine except for the path Beckett had cleared to the driveway. The sky was a brilliant blue that hurt her eyes, so different from Denver's hazy urban gray.

"I should read a book," she said aloud to the empty room. The thought surprised her. When was the last time she'd read something that wasn't a medical journal or hospital policy update?

She showered quickly, pulled her hair into its usual low bun, and headed downstairs. Her father sat at the kitchen table with a mug of coffee and the newspaper.

"Morning," he said, not looking up.

"Good morning." Tessa poured herself coffee from the pot. "Is Beckett around?"

"Hardware store. Something about a broken latch on the shed."

She nodded, though her father couldn't see it. "I

thought I might walk into town. Get some fresh air."

He folded the newspaper and looked at her then. "Supposed to be clear all day. Good day for a walk."

Was that approval in his voice? She couldn't tell. "Do you need anything before I go? Medication check or..."

He tapped his pill organizer on the table. "I'm all set. Beckett makes sure of it."

Of course he did. "Right. Well, I'll have my phone if you need me."

He nodded and returned to his paper. She hesitated, then grabbed her coat from the hook by the door and stepped outside.

The cold hit her lungs like a shock, clean and clarifying. She followed the shoveled sidewalk into town, her boots crunching in the snow. Sweet River Falls looked charming, with the storefronts decorated with garlands and lights, and smoke curling from chimneys. She'd forgotten how beautiful it could be.

She passed the town square, where a Christmas tree stood tall and bright even in daylight. A banner hung across Main Street announcing, "Sweet River Falls Welcomes You Home for the Holidays."

Home. The word caught in her throat.

She pushed into Bookish Cafe, and the warmth enveloped her immediately, along with the rich scent of coffee. The cafe was busier than she expected, with nearly every table occupied by people chatting over steaming mugs.

Annie looked up from behind the counter and waved. "Tessa! What a nice surprise. What can I get you?"

"Just coffee, black. And I thought I'd get a book while I'm here."

"Coming right up. And the new releases are on that shelf by the window."

She wandered over to the display and ran her fingers along the spines, reading titles that meant nothing to her. How had she fallen so out of touch with current books? There had been a time when she devoured novels, staying up late to finish just one more chapter.

"Here you go." Annie appeared at her side, holding out a large mug. "See anything that catches your eye?"

She accepted the coffee. "I honestly don't know where to start. It's been... a while since I've read for pleasure."

"Hospital work doesn't leave much time for that, does it?"

"No. Though that's not a great excuse."

"Well, let me help." Annie scanned the shelf and pulled out a paperback with a blue cover. "This one's gotten wonderful reviews. It's about a woman who inherits her grandmother's house in a small coastal town and discovers family secrets. A bit of mystery to it."

She took the book, flipping it over to read the back. "Sounds perfect, actually."

"Excellent choice," a deep voice said from behind her.

She turned to find Beckett standing there, a small paper bag in his hand. His cheeks were flushed from the cold, his eyes bright.

"You've read it?" she asked, surprised.

He nodded. "I read a lot these days. That one's good. Great mystery. The ending will surprise you."

Annie glanced between them, a small smile playing at her lips. "Beckett's one of my best customers. He's working his way through my entire fiction section."

"Just the good ones," he said with a slight shrug. "Stan asked me to pick up his medication while I was out. I should get back. Enjoy your book."

He nodded goodbye and headed for the door. She watched him go, noticing how several people called out greetings as he passed. He responded to each one with a quiet word or nod.

"He's really found his place here," Annie said, following her gaze.

She turned back to Annie. "It seems that way. Everyone treats him like he's lived here forever."

"That's Sweet River Falls for you. Once you're one of ours, you're family." Annie squeezed her arm. "That includes you too, you know. No matter how long you've been away."

She wasn't sure how to respond to that. She sipped her coffee instead.

"Actually," Annie said, "since you're here, I could use your help with something."

"Oh?"

"I'm decorating for our holiday reading night. My usual helper is down with the flu."

She glanced at her watch out of habit, then realized she had nowhere else to be. No shifts to cover, no patients waiting. Just time, stretching out empty before her.

"I'd be happy to help," she said.

"Wonderful! Let me just tell my worker at the counter, and we can head to the back."

While Annie spoke with the young woman behind the counter, she noticed a large corkboard near the register. It was covered in small pieces of paper in various colors, each pinned haphazardly across the surface. A sign above it read "Wish Notes" in flowing script.

She moved closer, reading a few of the notes.

"I wish for a new bike for my brother. His got stolen, and Mom says we can't afford another one."

"I wish my dad would come home for Christmas this year."

"I wish someone would notice me."

"I wish for one day without pain."

"I wish I could forget how much I miss you."

Each note was unsigned, anonymous wishes sent out into the universe. Some were hopeful, while others were heartbreaking in their simplicity.

"It's our annual tradition," Annie said, coming to stand beside her. "People write down their holiday wishes, and sometimes others in town make them come true. Anonymously, of course."

"That's beautiful." She stared at the corkboard.

"It started small, just a few wishes. Now we get hundreds." Annie pointed to a blue note near the bottom. "That little boy got his puppy last year. And this woman," she indicated a pink note, "received two months' worth of meals after her surgery."

She read more notes, feeling a tightness in her throat.

"I wish Mom would smile again."

"I wish for courage to start over."

"I wish to belong somewhere."

That last one hit her like an unexpected punch. How many times had she felt that exact sentiment, even in Denver, where she'd built her whole adult life?

"People think small towns are simple. But we hold just as much complexity as anywhere else. Pain and hope side by side."

She nodded, unable to speak for a moment.

"Come on," Annie said, touching her arm gently. "The decorations are in the storage room."

She followed her through a door behind the counter into a small hallway. Annie unlocked a door and flicked on the light, revealing a room lined with shelves stacked with boxes.

"These are the holiday ones," Annie said, pointing to a stack labeled in the corner. "We need the ones labeled Reading Night."

She pulled down the first box, surprised by its weight. "What's in here, bricks?"

Annie laughed. "Book-themed ornaments, mostly. And the fairy lights. Lots and lots of fairy lights."

They carried the boxes out to the main cafe area, where Annie had cleared a large table. As they unpacked, she found herself surrounded by tiny book ornaments, miniature reading lamps, and strings of lights shaped like open books.

"These are amazing," she said, holding up a tiny replica of *Pride and Prejudice*.

"I've collected them throughout the years," Annie explained, untangling a string of lights. "The reading night is my favorite event. We turn off all the regular lights and read by these fairy lights. Kids come in pajamas with their favorite books. It's magical."

She could almost picture it in her mind with the soft glow of lights, children curled up with books, and the warmth of community surrounding them. Something inside her ached at the image.

"Would you like to come?"

"I... maybe. I'm not sure how long I'll be staying."

Annie nodded, not pushing. "Well, the invitation stands. Now, can you help me hang these lights around the windows?"

For the next hour, they worked together, transforming the cafe into an even cozier space. Tessa climbed the ladder to hang lights while Annie directed from below. The physical activity felt good and purposeful in a different way than her hospital work.

As they finished, she found herself back at the wish board, drawn to the anonymous hopes and dreams of her hometown.

"Would you like to add one?" Annie asked, holding out a small green slip of paper and a pen.

She hesitated. What would she wish for? Health for her father seemed too obvious. A return to normal in Denver? But what was normal anymore? The panic attacks in supply closets? The trembling hands she tried to hide?

"Maybe later." She handed back the paper.

Annie nodded, understanding. "The board will be here when you're ready."

She paid for her book and thanked Annie for the coffee. As she prepared to leave, Annie called out, "Tessa, wait. I forgot to give you this."

She held out a small paper bag. "Blueberry

muffin. Will you give it to your dad? It's his favorite."

She took the bag. "Yes, I will. Thank you."

Outside, the temperature had dropped. She tucked the book and muffin into her coat and started the walk back to her father's house.

Her mind kept returning to those wish notes. All those quiet desires, some simple and some profound. It struck her that beneath the picture-perfect surface of Sweet River Falls, there was so much more happening. People struggling, hoping, dreaming, hurting. Just like anywhere else. Just like her.

She paused at the edge of town, looking back at the twinkling lights strung across Main Street. For the first time since arriving, she didn't feel quite so much like an outsider looking in. There was pain here, yes, but there was also hope. And maybe, there was room for her pain and her hope too.

The wish board had shown her that everyone had their own story and their own struggles hidden beneath the surface. Even Beckett, with his quiet strength and careful distance. Even her father, who had somehow changed enough to welcome a stranger into his home.

As she continued walking, snow beginning to fall in gentle flakes around her, she found herself wondering what Beckett might have wished for or what her father might write on one of those colored slips of paper. What would healing look like for each of them?

She didn't have answers, but the questions didn't fill her with dread. Instead, she felt a flicker of something that might have been curiosity. Or perhaps, more dangerously, it might have been hope.

CHAPTER 9

Tessa settled onto the couch with a quilt tucked around her legs. The house had grown quiet after her father headed to bed early. She'd checked his vitals and made sure he took his evening medication before he shuffled off to his bedroom. Now the only sounds were the occasional pop from the fireplace and the soft ticking of the old clock on the mantel.

She should be tired. Her body felt heavy with exhaustion, but her mind refused to slow down. Too many thoughts competed for her attention. Her father's health. The town's unexpected welcome. The way Beckett seemed to fit so seamlessly into life here in Sweet River Falls. A life that somehow felt like it should have been hers if she'd wanted it. But, of course, she hadn't. She'd run away from town as fast as she could after high school graduation.

The front door opened, bringing with it a gust of cold air and the subject of her thoughts. Beckett stomped his boots on the mat before stepping inside, his cheeks ruddy from the cold.

He unwound his scarf. "It's really coming down now. We might have another six inches by morning."

She nodded, watching as he hung his coat on the hook by the door. The same row of hooks where her father had always hung his jacket. Where her mother's raincoat had once hung. It was strange how such small things could feel so significant.

"Stan get to bed okay?" he asked, rubbing his hands together to warm them.

"Yes. He was tired and went to bed early with a fishing magazine."

He glanced toward the kitchen. "I was thinking of making some hot chocolate to warm up. Would you like some?"

"Sure," she said after a moment. "That sounds nice."

He disappeared into the kitchen, and she listened to the familiar sounds of cupboards opening and closing, the clink of mugs, the quiet efficiency of someone who knew their way around her father's kitchen better than she did.

When he returned, he carried two steaming mugs. He handed one to her before taking a seat in the armchair across from the couch. The chocolate was rich and dark, with a hint of cinnamon that reminded her of her mother's recipe.

"This is good. Did my dad teach you how to make this?"

A small smile crossed his face. "No. Miss Judy at the lodge showed me. She said it was your mother's recipe."

The revelation sent a pang through her chest. "My mother's recipe?"

"Stan mentioned it once when we were at the lodge for dinner. Miss Judy insisted on teaching me."

She took another sip, letting the warmth spread through her. Her mother's hot chocolate. Another piece of her that had somehow survived all these years, passed along to others without her knowing. Passed along to Beckett, not her.

"How long have you known my father?" she asked abruptly.

He seemed to consider the question. "About seven months now. I moved in six months ago, but I met him before that."

"And you just... moved in with a stranger?"

"Your father volunteered to be a sponsor."

It was hard for her to fathom. The Stan Grant she knew kept to himself. He didn't invite people in. He certainly didn't volunteer to help strangers. "I don't understand why he would do that."

Beckett was quiet for a long moment, as if weighing what to say next. "Maybe he was lonely."

The simple statement hit her harder than she expected. Had her father been lonely? She'd never considered it. In her mind, he'd always been self-sufficient, preferring his solitude. But what if that wasn't true? What if he'd just never known how to reach out?

"You said reentry program," she said, latching onto the practical rather than the emotional. "So you were..."

"In prison. Yes." He said it plainly, without defensiveness or shame. Just a statement of fact.

She'd assumed as much from what Annie had said, but hearing him confirm it was different. She paused, then plunged ahead. "For what?"

"Accessory to armed robbery."

She blinked, not expecting such a direct answer. "That sounds serious."

"It was." He picked up his mug again, wrapping his hands around it as if drawing strength from its warmth. "I made a mistake when I was younger. A big one. I trusted the wrong person, and I paid for it with fifteen years of my life."

"What happened?" she asked, surprised by her own curiosity.

Beckett took a deep breath. "My father died when I was nineteen. Heart attack. It was unexpected, and I... didn't handle it well."

Something in his tone made her look at him more closely. There was a familiar pain there, one she recognized.

"First, I started getting into minor trouble, then I went a bit wild," he continued. "Started hanging out with a different crowd. One of them was a guy named Mitchell. He seemed to understand what I was going through. His own father had died a few years earlier."

He paused, taking a sip of his hot chocolate. "We became friends. Or at least I thought we were friends. One night, he asked me to drive him to a convenience store. Said his car was in the shop and he needed to pick something up."

She could guess where this was going, but she remained silent, letting him tell his story.

"I waited in the car. Had no idea what he was planning. Then I heard shouting, and Mitchell came running out with a gun in his hand." His voice remained steady, but she could see the tension in his shoulders. "He jumped in the car and told me to drive. I panicked. Did what he said."

"What happened next?"

"We were caught about an hour later. The clerk had been shot, but thankfully survived. Mitchell claimed I was in on it from the beginning. That I was the mastermind." A humorless smile crossed his face. "The jury believed him. He had a better lawyer, a cleaner record. I got fifteen years. He got seven."

She studied him across the space between them. His face was open and unguarded. There was no plea for sympathy in his eyes, just a quiet acceptance.

He met her gaze directly. "Anyway, you deserve to know who's living in your father's house. I'm not hiding who I am or what I did. Or more accurately, what I failed to do."

"What you failed to do?"

"I failed to see Mitchell for who he really was. I failed to stop the robbery. I failed to make better choices." He set his mug down again. "But I served my time. I've spent the last fifteen years trying to become someone my father would have been proud of, even if I was inside prison walls."

The conviction in his voice was unmistakable. Whatever else Beckett Cole might be, he wasn't trying to escape his past or pretend it hadn't happened.

"I understand grief," he said more softly. "I understand how it can change a person. Make them shut down when they should open up. Make them push away the people they need the most."

The words struck too close to home. She looked away, focusing on the dancing flames in the fire-place. "Is that what you think happened with my father and me?"

"I think grief affects everyone differently. And sometimes it's easier to blame the living than to accept that the dead are really gone."

She felt a lump forming in her throat. "You don't know anything about my relationship with my father."

"You're right," he agreed readily. "I don't. But I do know Stan. And I know he keeps your graduation photo on his nightstand. I know he saves every card you send him in a box in his closet. I know he watches for the mail carrier on his birthday, Christmas, and Father's Day, hoping for something from you."

Each word was like a small stone dropping into still water, creating ripples that disturbed the surface of everything she thought she knew.

"I'm not telling you this to make you feel guilty. I'm telling you because I think you should know that whatever happened between you two, he never stopped caring."

She wrapped her hands tighter around her mug, trying to ground herself in its solid warmth. "After my mom died, he just... shut down. It was like he couldn't see me anymore. Like I wasn't enough."

The admission surprised her. She hadn't meant to say it out loud, hadn't meant to reveal that old, deep hurt to this stranger.

"I doubt that was it. From what I've seen, Stan

isn't good at showing what he feels. But that doesn't mean he doesn't feel it."

"You sound like you know him pretty well."

He shrugged slightly. "We're both men who made mistakes and lost years we can't get back."

The parallel hadn't occurred to her before. Her father had lost years to grief just as surely as Beckett had lost years to prison.

"I'm not asking for your trust, Tessa. I know I haven't earned it. But I wanted you to know the truth about me. No secrets, no surprises."

She studied him, this quiet man with his steady gaze and careful words. There was something solid about him, a groundedness that seemed at odds with the story he'd just told. "Thank you for telling me. I appreciate your honesty."

He nodded, accepting her response without pushing for more. They sat in silence for a while, finishing their hot chocolate as the fire crackled and the snow fell outside.

"I should probably turn in. Morning comes early," Beckett said eventually, rising from his chair.

"Do you always get up at dawn to shovel snow?"

A small smile crossed his face. "Only when it snows."

"Which seems to be every day in December."

His smile widened slightly. "Welcome back to Sweet River Falls, where winter is a commitment, not a season."

The familiar local saying surprised a laugh out of her. "I'd forgotten about that."

He collected their empty mugs. "Good night, Tessa."

"Night, Beckett."

She watched as he carried the mugs to the kitchen, his footsteps quiet and measured. After he disappeared down the hallway to his room, she remained on the couch, staring at the dying fire.

Fifteen years in prison for a mistake made in grief. It seemed an impossibly harsh punishment. Yet Beckett didn't seem bitter or angry. He just seemed determined to move forward, to rebuild his life one careful step at a time.

Tessa pulled the quilt tighter around her shoulders. She'd come back to Sweet River Falls expecting to find her father unchanged and the town frozen in time like her memories. Instead, she'd found everything altered. Her father was softer, more connected to the community. The town was thriving and welcoming. And now there was Beckett, with his quiet strength and unexpected honesty.

She thought about what he'd said about grief, about pushing away the people you need most. Had she done that? Had her father? They'd both been so wounded by her mother's death that they'd retreated into themselves.

Maybe they'd been more alike than different all along.

Outside, the snow continued to fall, covering Sweet River Falls in a blanket of white that muffled sound and transformed the familiar into something new and beautiful. She watched it through the window, feeling something shift inside her. Not forgiveness, not yet. But perhaps the beginning of understanding.

CHAPTER 10

TESSA WOKE to the soft sound of voices drifting down the hallway. She blinked at the ceiling, momentarily disoriented by the familiarity of her childhood bedroom. The pale winter sunlight filtered through the curtains. She sat up and stretched.

Fourteen days. She'd been back in Sweet River Falls for two whole weeks now. The realization startled her. Somehow, the time had slipped by in a rhythm that felt both foreign and strangely comfortable. Each morning, she checked her father's vitals and medications. Each afternoon, she found herself either helping with small tasks around town or reading in the quiet of the living room. And each evening...

Each evening, she and Beckett ended up by the fireplace, talking until the embers died down.

She swung her legs over the side of the bed, surprised at how easily she'd fallen into this pattern. In Denver, her life had been a constant rush of emergencies and overtime shifts, collapsing into bed only to wake and do it all again. Here, time moved differently. The pace was slower, but somehow she felt more awake than she had in years.

She found her father and Beckett at the kitchen table, the paper spread between them.

"Morning," she said, heading for the coffee pot.

Her father looked up, his reading glasses perched on the end of his nose. "There you are. Been wondering when you'd join the land of the living."

The comment might have stung a week ago, but she'd begun to recognize the gruff affection beneath her father's words. "It's barely eight o'clock, Dad."

"Eight-fifteen," he corrected, tapping his watch. "Beckett's already fixed the loose step on the back porch and cleared the walkway."

"Sorry, I missed all the excitement," she said, but without the edge that would have colored her words when she first arrived.

Beckett glanced up from the paper, the corners of his eyes crinkling. "Don't worry. I saved some excitement for you. The kitchen sink is still dripping. And we need a five-letter word for happy." He motioned to the crossword puzzle in the paper.

"Jolly."

Her father shook his head.

"Merry."

"That works." Her father scribbled the answer on the puzzle.

She found herself smiling as she poured her coffee. This too had become part of their routine, the gentle teasing and the way Beckett deflected her father's occasional sharpness.

Later, Beckett went out to run errands, and she cleaned up the cottage, then settled down to read her book. Beckett came back to the cabin, stamping the snow off his boots. "Coming down hard now. Main Street is emptying out. People are heading home. Kind of pretty out, though."

Her father got up and looked out the window. "Looks like at least seven or eight more inches since this morning. It's perfect for walking the River Walk."

She frowned. "You want to walk the River Walk? Dad, I don't think that's a good idea yet. Your blood pressure—"

Her father waved a dismissive hand. "Not me. You two. You and Beckett."

The suggestion hung in the air. She glanced at Beckett, whose expression remained carefully neutral.

"I used to take you when you were little," her father continued, his voice softening with memory.

"After a fresh snow. You'd run ahead, making those little footprints all over the pristine white."

Something caught in her throat. She remembered those walks, her mother bundling her in a red coat and matching mittens, her father lifting her onto his shoulders when her legs grew tired.

"I don't know, Dad. I should probably stay here with you."

Her father fixed her with a look. "I'm not an invalid, Tessa. Doc says I'm making good progress. Besides, Ronnie's coming over to play cards. He'll be here any minute."

"Ronnie from the B&B? I met his wife, Lucy, when we were working on the food baskets. But since when do you play cards with Ronnie?"

"Since I got tired of losing to Beckett," her father said with a wry smile. "Go on. Fresh air will do you good."

She looked at Beckett again. "What do you think?"

"I think the River Walk is beautiful after a fresh snow."

A half-hour later, bundled in a coat and scarf, she walked beside Beckett. He had been right. It appeared most people had cleared out of town and headed back to their homes to wait out the storm. Annie had even closed Bookish Cafe early.

They walked along the path that wound behind

Main Street. The River Walk had changed since her childhood, with new benches and decorative lights strung through the trees, but the rushing water of Sweet River remained the same, partially frozen at the edges, flowing strong in the center.

Their boots crunched in the untouched snow. She breathed deeply, the cold air sharp in her lungs.

"Dad was right. This is perfect."

He nodded, his breath forming clouds in the air. "I come here a lot. To think."

"What do you think about?" The question slipped out before she could consider it.

He was quiet for a long moment, and she wondered if she'd crossed some invisible line. But then he spoke, his voice low and steady.

"Everything. The past. The future. How different they look from what I expected."

She nodded, understanding that feeling all too well. "I never expected to be back here. I was so sure I'd built the perfect life in Denver."

"And had you?"

The question was gentle, but it hit her hard. Had she? The long shifts, the empty apartment, and the growing sense of disconnect from her patients and colleagues...

"I thought I had." She shrugged. "Until I didn't."

They walked in silence for a while, the only

sounds the crunch of snow beneath their feet and the rushing water beside them. Ahead, the path curved around a stand of pines, their branches heavy with white.

"Can I ask you something?" she said.

He nodded.

"How did you... I mean, after everything that happened to you, how did you find your way back?"

He considered her question carefully. "In prison, I had a lot of time to think. Too much, sometimes. I was angry at first. At my friend, at the system, and at myself most of all."

"What changed?"

"There was a woodworking program taught by an old man named Joe. He'd been a master carpenter before he retired. Volunteered at the prison twice a week."

They reached a bench overlooking a small bend in the river. Beckett brushed away the snow and gestured for her to sit. The wood was cold beneath her, but the view was worth it, the mountains rising beyond the town, majestic and eternal.

"Joe taught me how to see the potential in a piece of wood. How to be patient and to work with the grain instead of against it. He used to say that every mistake was just an opportunity to create something different than what you planned."

"Sounds like a wise man."

"He was. He also told me that forgiveness wasn't

about the other person. It was about freeing your-self." He paused and looked out at the river. "That was harder to learn than the woodworking."

Snowflakes drifted down around them. One landed on her eyelash, and she blinked it away. "Have you? Forgiven yourself?"

"Some days. Other days, I still wonder what my life would have been if I'd made different choices. If I hadn't gotten in that car."

The vulnerability in his admission touched something in her. Here was someone who under-stood what it meant to question the path you'd taken and wonder about the roads not traveled.

"I think about my past every day," he added quietly. "Not just the bad parts, but all of it. The good choices, the bad ones. The people who helped me, and the ones who didn't. It's all part of who I am now."

She nodded, watching the snowflakes disappear into the rushing water. "I used to be so sure about who I was. Tessa Grant, ER nurse. Responsible. Reliable. Always the one who could handle the crisis."

"And now?"

She pulled her scarf tighter. "Now I'm not sure who I am without work and responsibility. I've built my whole identity around being needed and being the capable one. And then suddenly..."

"Suddenly what?"

She hadn't told anyone about the panic attacks. To her co-workers, she'd cited exhaustion, burnout, and the standard excuses that wouldn't raise too many questions. But sitting here with Beckett, with the snow falling around them and no expectations pressing down, the truth felt less frightening.

"I started having panic attacks." The words came out in a rush. "At work. The first one happened during a trauma case. Multiple car accident, three critical patients. The kind of situation I'd handled dozens of times before."

She stared at her gloved hands. "I couldn't breathe. Couldn't think. Had to hide in the supply closet until it passed. After that, they kept happening. My hands would shake when I tried to insert IVs. I'd forget basic protocols I'd known for years."

Saying it aloud made it real in a way it hadn't been before, even to herself. "I'm not sure I can go back to ER work. And if I can't do that... I don't know who I am."

The confession hung between them, as real as the snowflakes drifting down. She waited for the judgment, the platitudes, and the well-meaning advice she'd expected from anyone she told.

Instead, he simply nodded. "I understand that. When everything you thought defined you is suddenly gone, it's like standing on the edge of a cliff."

"Exactly," she whispered, relief washing through her at being understood.

"But maybe…" He paused and looked at her. "There's freedom in that too. In being able to redefine yourself."

She considered his words. "Is that what you did?"

"I'm still doing it. Every day. Some days are better than others."

A cardinal landed on a branch nearby, dislodging a small shower of snow. They both watched as it flitted away, leaving the branch bobbing gently.

"Can I tell you something I've never told anyone?" he asked.

She nodded, touched by his willingness to share with her.

"When I first got out, I was terrified of open spaces. Sounds strange, I know, but after fifteen years of walls and fences and limited horizons... suddenly having all that space, all those choices, it was overwhelming."

"What did you do?"

"I found one small thing I could manage each day. Making my bed. Walking to the end of the block and back. Cooking a meal from scratch." He smiled slightly. "Gradually, the world got bigger, and I got braver."

She thought about her own fears, how overwhelming the hospital had become, how even the thought of returning made her heart race. "One small thing at a time," she repeated.

"It's not a cure, but it helps."

They sat in companionable silence as the snow continued to fall, dusting their shoulders and hair. She found herself studying Beckett's profile, the strong line of his jaw, and the thoughtfulness in his eyes. How strange that this man, whom she'd initially resented as an intruder in her father's house, now felt like the person who best understood her.

"We should head back," she said eventually. "Before Dad sends out a search party."

He stood and offered his hand. She took it, surprised by the warmth that spread through her gloved fingers at his touch. He helped her up, and for a moment, they stood close enough that she could see the individual snowflakes landing on his shoulders.

"Thank you," she said.

"For what?"

"For listening. For understanding. For not trying to fix me."

Something shifted in his expression, a softening around the eyes. "You don't need fixing, Tessa."

The walk back was quieter, but the silence felt comfortable and filled with unspoken understanding rather than awkwardness. The snow fell heavier now, transforming Sweet River Falls into a winter wonderland. Christmas lights twinkled from shop windows, and the scent of pine and smoke from the chimneys filled the air.

As they approached her father's house, she realized she felt lighter somehow, as if sharing her fears had diminished their power. The panic that had been her constant companion in Denver seemed distant here, replaced by something she couldn't quite name. Not happiness exactly, but perhaps the possibility of it.

Through the window of the cabin, she could see her father laughing at something, cards spread on the table between him and Ronnie. The sight warmed her more than she expected.

"They seem to be having fun," she observed.

He nodded. "Your dad and Ronnie seem to really enjoy their card nights."

They stood at the edge of the yard, snow gathering on their shoulders, neither quite ready to go inside and break the spell of understanding that had formed between them.

"Do you think you'll stay in Sweet River Falls?" she asked suddenly. "After your program ends?"

He brushed snow from his sleeve, considering. "I'd like to. It feels like somewhere I could belong." He looked at her. "What about you? Will you go back to Denver?"

The question caught her off guard. A week ago,

she would have answered without hesitation. Of course, she would go back. Her life was there, her career, her apartment. But now...

"I don't know," she admitted. "I thought I knew exactly what I wanted. Now I'm not so sure."

He nodded, understanding in his eyes. "Sometimes the hardest paths to see are the ones right in front of us."

A gust of wind swirled snow around them, and she shivered despite her layers.

"We should go in. You're cold."

"Just a minute more." She wanted to hold onto this moment, this connection, for just a little longer. "It's beautiful out here."

And it was. The snow-covered yard, the lights glowing from within the house, and the mountains rising beyond the town, solid and reassuring. For the first time since arriving in Sweet River Falls, she felt something like peace settle over her.

"What are you thinking?" he asked softly.

She turned to him. "That I'm glad I came home." She surprised herself with the truth of it. "Even if I didn't want to at first."

Something warm flickered in his eyes. "I'm glad you did too."

For a moment, she thought he might reach for her hand again, and part of her hoped he would. Instead, he gestured toward the house. "Shall we?"

As they walked up the steps to the front door,

their footprints side by side in the fresh snow, she realized she had found something unexpected. She had found a connection with someone who saw her clearly, flaws and fears and all, and still wanted to walk beside her.

CHAPTER 11

Tessa had almost forgotten what it felt like to anticipate something. For months in Denver, her days had blurred into an endless cycle of hospital shifts and restless sleep. But this morning, she found herself looking forward to helping Annie with the children's reading night at Bookish Cafe.

She pulled on her boots and went into the kitchen, surprised to find the house quiet. Her father was at his weekly doctor's appointment, with Beckett driving him. The silence felt strange after nearly two weeks of their constant presence.

In the kitchen, she found a note from Beckett in his neat handwriting: "Taking your dad to Dr. Miller. Back around noon. Coffee's fresh."

The thoughtfulness of the gesture made her smile. When had Beckett Cole started to matter so much? She poured herself a cup and wrapped her hands around the warm mug, savoring the moment of peace.

The walk to Bookish Cafe took her past snow-covered storefronts decorated for Christmas. Sweet River Falls looked like a postcard, pristine and perfect. But she knew better now. Beneath the twinkling lights and wreaths, people carried their own struggles. The wish notes at Annie's had shown her that.

Annie was arranging books on a display table when Tessa pushed open the door.

"Perfect timing," Annie called. "I just finished setting up the reading corner. We need to hang the paper snowflakes the kids made last week."

She hung her coat and scarf on the rack by the door. "Put me to work."

For the next hour, they transformed the children's corner into a winter wonderland, hanging delicate paper snowflakes from fishing line and arranging cushions in a semicircle around a rocking chair.

She stepped back to admire their work. "This looks magical. The kids will love it."

"Speaking of magical," Annie said, "I saw you and Beckett walking on the River Walk the other day."

Heat crept into her cheeks. "We were just getting some fresh air."

"Mmhmm." Annie's knowing smile made her blush harder.

"It's not like that," she insisted, though she wasn't entirely convinced herself. Something had shifted between them during that snowy walk. The way he'd listened when she told him about her panic attacks and offered understanding instead of solutions. The way he'd trusted her with his own fears.

"He's good people, you know. What he did all those years ago... it doesn't define who he is now."

"I know," she said, and realized she meant it.

"Well, I need more coffee before I tackle the next task. Want some?"

"Sure."

While Annie prepared fresh cups, Tessa wandered over to the community bulletin board. The colorful wish notes were still there, alongside flyers for the Christmas festivals and local business advertisements. She scanned the board, smiling at a child's handwritten wish for a puppy.

Then her eyes caught on a note she hadn't seen before. Unlike the cheerful colored papers of the wish notes, this one was stark white, and the message was typed rather than handwritten.

"You can put up lights and bake cookies, but you can't wash away a prison record."

Her stomach clenched. She read it again,

hoping she'd misunderstood, but the words remained unchanged. Cold. Deliberate.

"Annie, did you see this?"

Annie appeared at her side, coffee mugs in hand. Her eyes widened as she read the note. "No. Oh no." She quickly snatched it off the board. "I wonder how long it's been up there. I didn't notice it."

Her hands curled into fists. "It's about Beckett, isn't it?"

Annie nodded, her expression grim. "There are still a few people in town who aren't happy about the reentry program. Walter Dobbs has been particularly vocal."

"Walter Dobbs?"

"He's a grumpy old man who thinks people can't change. He also likes to stir up trouble." Annie crumpled the note. "I thought this kind of thing had stopped months ago."

She took the crumpled paper from Annie's hand and smoothed it out. "Has Beckett seen notes like this before?"

"A few, when he first came to town. But it's been quiet lately. I thought people had finally accepted him. He never complained, just kept his head down and worked harder."

Of course, he had. Beckett wasn't the type to draw attention to himself or his troubles. He'd endure this silently too, just as he'd endured fifteen years in prison for a crime he hadn't actually committed.

"Who else knows about his past?" she asked.

"Most of the town, I suppose. It's not exactly a secret in a place this small. Not the details, but the fact he's been in prison. But most folks have come around. They've seen how he is with your dad, how he teaches those woodworking classes at the community center, and how he's always the first to volunteer when someone needs help."

She thought about Beckett shoveling snow before dawn, the careful way he tracked her father's medication, and his quiet presence that somehow made the house feel more like home than it had in years.

"This isn't right." Anger swelled inside her.

"No, it's not. But the best thing we can do is ignore it. Don't give whoever wrote this the satisfaction."

She wasn't so sure. Part of her wanted to march up to Walter Dobbs and confront him. But another part of her, the part that had spent the last two weeks observing Beckett, knew that wasn't what he would want.

"I should get back. Dad and Beckett will be home soon."

Annie hesitated, then asked, "Are you going to tell him?"

"I don't know." She carefully folded the note

and slipped it into her pocket. "Maybe he doesn't need to know."

But as she walked home through the snow, she couldn't shake the sick feeling in her stomach. Not just anger at whoever had written the note, but something else. Something that felt uncomfortably like guilt.

Because hadn't she done the same thing when she first arrived? Judged Beckett based on his past, on the single fact that he'd been in prison? She'd been suspicious and standoffish, quick to question his place in her father's home.

The realization made her steps falter. She'd been no better than whoever wrote that note.

When she reached the house, she found her father and Beckett already back. Stan was napping in his recliner, and Beckett was in the kitchen preparing lunch.

"How was the appointment?" she asked, hanging her coat by the door.

"Good. Dr. Miller says his blood pressure is improving." Beckett glanced up from the cutting board where he was slicing vegetables for a salad. "How was Annie's?"

"Fine. We got everything ready for the reading night." She hesitated, the folded note heavy in her pocket. "The cafe looks great."

He nodded, returning his attention to the

vegetables. There was something in his posture, a tension that hadn't been there during their walk the other day.

"Is everything okay?" she asked.

"Sure." But he didn't meet her eyes.

Her heart sank. He already knew. Somehow, he already knew about the note.

"Beckett..."

"Your dad should eat soon," he said, still not looking at her. "The appointment tired him out."

She watched as he efficiently assembled sandwiches and salad, his movements precise and controlled. Too controlled. Like someone working very hard to appear normal.

"I saw the note," she blurted out. "At Annie's. On the bulletin board."

His hands stilled for just a moment before resuming their work. "It's nothing."

"It's not nothing. It's cruel and unfair."

He shrugged, a small, tight movement. "It happens."

"It shouldn't."

"No," he agreed quietly. "But it does."

She moved closer, until she was standing beside him at the counter. "Has this happened before?"

"A few times when I first got here." He finally looked at her, his gray-blue eyes carefully neutral. "It's been a while."

"Who do you think wrote it?"

"Does it matter?"

"Yes," she insisted. "It matters."

He set down the knife and faced her fully. "Why? What would you do if you knew?"

The question caught her off guard. What would she do? Confront them? Demand an apology? And then what?

"I don't know," she admitted. "But it's wrong. You don't deserve that."

Something flickered across his face, too quick to read. "It's okay, Tessa. I've dealt with worse."

The quiet resignation in his voice broke something inside her. She thought about all he'd endured. Fifteen years in prison. Starting over with nothing. And now this. "It's not okay. And you shouldn't have to just accept it."

"What's the alternative? Make a scene? Prove them right about me?" He turned back to the lunch preparation.

"They're not right about you."

He looked at her then, really looked at her, and the vulnerability in his eyes made her breath catch. "Weren't you thinking the same thing when you first got here? That I was dangerous? That I didn't belong in your father's house?"

The truth of his words stung. She had thought exactly that. She had resented his presence and questioned his motives. She had seen the ex-con instead of the man.

"Yes, I did. And I was wrong," she admitted.

He seemed surprised by her candor.

"I judged you without knowing you, and that was unfair. But I know you now, Beckett. I've seen how you are with my dad and with the town. You're a good man."

He looked away, uncomfortable with her praise. "We should get your dad up for lunch."

But she wasn't ready to let it go. "Why didn't you tell me about the note?"

He sighed. "What good would it do? Some people won't ever see past what I did. I've accepted that."

"Well, I haven't. And you shouldn't either."

"Tessa." His voice was gentle but firm. "This isn't your battle."

"Maybe it should be." The words surprised her as much as they seemed to surprise him. "Maybe it's time someone fought for you for a change."

Their eyes met, and something shifted in the air between them. Something warm and electric that made her heart beat faster.

"Why would you do that?" he asked softly.

Because I care about you, she wanted to say. Because you deserve better. Because when I'm with you, I feel more like myself than I have in years.

But before she could find the words, her father called from the living room, breaking the moment.

"Lunch ready yet? I'm starving out here."

Beckett stepped back, and the connection between them faded as quickly as it had formed. "Coming right up," he called.

He turned to grab plates from the cabinet, his expression once again carefully neutral. "We should get him in the kitchen for lunch."

She nodded, frustrated by the interruption but knowing this wasn't the time to press. She went to get her father and helped him settle at the kitchen table. Beckett put the food on the table.

"About time," Stan grumbled, though there was no real heat in his words. "Doctor visits always make me hungry."

She handed him his plate, studying him closely. "Everything okay at the appointment?"

He waved dismissively. "Fine, fine. Blood pressure's down. Doc says I'm doing good."

"That's great, Dad."

They ate in relative silence, Stan occasionally commenting on the food or asking about her morning at the cafe. She answered automatically, her mind still on Beckett and the note. He was quieter than usual, focusing on his food and avoiding her gaze.

After lunch, Beckett excused himself to work on some project in the garage. She helped her father settle back into his recliner with a magazine before cleaning up the kitchen.

Through the window, she could see Beckett in the detached garage, the door open despite the cold. He was standing at a workbench, methodically sanding a piece of wood. His face was set in concentration, but even from a distance, she could see the tension in his shoulders.

The unfairness of it all made her angry all over again. Here was a man who had lost fifteen years of his life for a mistake, who had rebuilt himself from nothing, and who gave so much to others without asking for anything in return. And someone in this town thought he deserved to be publicly shamed.

Worse, she had been part of the problem. She'd been quick to judge him based on his past and slow to see the man he'd become. The realization made her stomach twist with shame.

When the kitchen was clean, she checked on her father, who was dozing with the magazine resting on his lap. She grabbed her coat and headed to the garage.

The cold air hit her as she crossed the short distance between the house and the garage. Inside, the space was neat and organized, tools hanging on pegboards, and wood stacked carefully against one wall. Beckett looked up as she entered, his expression guarded.

"Need something?" he asked.

"Just wanted to see what you're working on."

He gestured to the piece of wood in front of him. "Jewelry box. For Miss Judy's granddaughter. I do small projects to earn some cash."

She moved closer to examine it. The wood was smooth and golden, the edges precisely mitered. "It's beautiful."

"Thanks." He resumed sanding, his movements rhythmic and practiced.

She watched him work for a moment, gathering her courage. "I'm sorry," she finally said.

He looked up, his forehead creased. "For what?"

"For how I acted when I first got here. For assuming the worst about you."

His hands stilled. "You didn't know me."

"That's no excuse." She met his eyes directly. "I'm a nurse. I should know better than to judge someone based on a single fact about their life."

He set down the sandpaper, his expression softening. "It's okay, Tessa. Really."

She took a deep breath. "No, it's not. And neither is that note. You deserve better. From this town, and from me."

Something vulnerable flickered in his eyes before he looked away. "I appreciate that."

They stood in silence for a moment, the only sound the soft whisper of snowfall outside the open garage door.

"You know," she said finally, "my mom used to

say that people show who they really are through their actions, not their words."

He looked up at her, waiting.

"Your actions show exactly who you are, Beckett. Someone who cares. Someone who helps. Someone worth knowing. Don't let anyone make you think otherwise."

The corner of his mouth lifted slightly, not quite a smile but close. "Your mom sounds like she was pretty wise."

"She was." She smiled, feeling the familiar ache of missing her mother, but it was softer now, less raw. "I think she would have liked you."

This time, his smile was real, if brief. "I would have liked to meet her."

"I wish you could have too," she said softly. "And I meant what I said earlier. About fighting for you. You shouldn't have to face this alone."

He looked at her for a long moment, and there was something unreadable in his expression. "Thank you. But I don't want to cause trouble. Especially not for you and your dad."

"It's not trouble to stand up for what's right."

Before he could respond, they heard Stan calling from the house. Beckett set down his tools immediately, always attentive to her father's needs.

As they walked back to the house together, she made a silent promise to herself. She wouldn't let Beckett face this alone, whether he wanted her help or not. Because somewhere along the way, this quiet, thoughtful man had become important to her. More important than she was ready to admit, even to herself.

And if someone in Sweet River Falls wanted to judge him for his past, they'd have to go through her first.

CHAPTER 12

TESSA ADJUSTED her festive red scarf and rubbed her gloved hands together as she surveyed the Christmas market taking shape around her. Sweet River Falls's town square had transformed overnight into a winter wonderland, with white twinkling lights strung between lampposts and evergreen garlands wrapped around anything that didn't move. Vendors hustled to set up their booths before the official opening in thirty minutes, their breath visible in the crisp morning air.

"Perfect timing," Annie called, waving from her Bookish Cafe booth. "I could use those extra hands."

She walked up to Annie's booth. "What do you need me to do?" She eyed the half-assembled display of holiday-themed books and the large coffee dispenser that needed setting up.

"Could you arrange those books while I finish with the coffee station? The Christmas romances sell like crazy this time of year." Annie pointed to several stacks of books with festive covers.

She picked up a book with a snow-covered cabin on the cover. "People really read these?"

Annie laughed. "Oh, honey. They can't get enough of them. Something about the holidays makes everyone want a happy ending."

As she arranged the books by color and size, creating an inviting display, she found herself smiling at the predictable but charming titles: Mistletoe Magic, Christmas at the Lighthouse, The Holiday Swap. She hadn't been much of a reader in recent years, but there was something comforting about these books with their promises of holiday cheer and guaranteed happy endings.

"There you go," she said, stepping back to admire her work. "The holiday books are all set."

"You've got quite the eye for display." Annie glanced at her watch. "I'm just going to pop over and speak to the festival coordinator. Back in a flash."

Tessa adjusted the handwritten price tag on a jar of Annie's hot chocolate mix and stepped back to survey the display. The Bookish Cafe booth looked festive and inviting, with twinkling lights strung along the awning and the stacks of holiday-themed books arranged beside specialty coffees and home-made treats.

Annie returned to the booth. "It looks great. I really appreciate the help." Annie poured each of them a steaming cup of hot chocolate. "We've got fifteen minutes before the official opening. Just enough time for a quick break."

She accepted the cup gratefully, wrapping her gloved hands around its warmth. The morning air was crisp and cold, and her breath formed little clouds that dissipated in the winter sunshine. All along Main Street, other vendors were putting final touches on their booths, creating a bustling energy in the town square.

"I forgot how beautiful this all is," she admitted, taking in the garlands of pine strung between lamp-posts and the enormous Christmas tree standing proud in the town square. "Denver does Christmas big, but it's all so commercial. This feels..."

"Like home?" Annie suggested with a knowing smile.

She didn't answer immediately. Was Sweet River Falls still home? The word felt complicated now, loaded with memories both painful and precious. Yet standing here in the heart of town, surrounded by familiar faces and traditions, she couldn't deny the pull she felt.

"Maybe," she finally said. "Parts of it, anyway."

Annie squeezed her arm. "That's a start."

Across the market, she spotted Beckett helping Nora set up the Sweet River Lodge booth. He worked methodically, arranging wooden ornaments on a display rack while Nora chattered away beside him. Even from this distance, she could see the tension in his shoulders and the careful way he kept his head down.

He'd been like that for days now, ever since the note. Their easy conversations had dried up, replaced by polite but distant exchanges. He left rooms when she entered them and made excuses about projects that needed attention. The connection they'd been building had fractured, and she felt its absence like a physical ache.

"Has he said anything to you?" Tessa asked, nodding toward Beckett.

Annie followed her gaze. "Not directly. But Nora mentioned he's been spending more time at the lodge workshop. Said he's making Christmas gifts."

"At least he's still showing up. That takes courage." She took a sip of her hot chocolate.

"More than most people have," Annie agreed. "Your father told me Beckett was thinking of leaving town after his program ends next month."

The news hit her like a punch to the stomach. "He never mentioned that to me."

"Maybe he doesn't want to," Annie said gently.

"Sometimes it's easier to slip away without goodbyes."

Before she could respond, the town bell rang out, signaling the market's opening. Almost immediately, shoppers began flowing into the square, bringing with them laughter and holiday cheer.

"Tessa Grant. Is that you?"

She turned to find Mrs. Hughes, her high school English teacher, beaming at her. The woman looked exactly the same, down to her silver-rimmed glasses and colorful scarf.

"Mrs. Hughes! It's so good to see you." And it was, she realized. There was something comforting about being recognized and having history in a place.

"I heard you were back in town. How wonderful that you're here for the holidays." Mrs. Hughes accepted a cup of peppermint hot chocolate from Annie. "We're all so proud of you, you know. Our hometown girl saving lives in the big city."

She felt a flush of embarrassment mixed with something like pride. "Oh, I'm just doing my job."

"Nonsense. It takes a special person to do what you do." Mrs. Hughes patted her arm. "Your mother would have been so proud."

The mention of her mother should have stung, but instead, it warmed her. "Thank you. That means a lot."

As Mrs. Hughes moved on, Tessa found herself

smiling. Throughout the morning, similar encounters repeated themselves. People she hadn't seen in years stopped by, not just for coffee and books, but to say hello, to welcome her back, to tell her they'd heard about her nursing career. Some asked about her father's health, expressing genuine concern.

For the next few hours, she found herself too busy to dwell on thoughts of Beckett's potential departure. She rang up purchases, wrapped books in festive paper, and chatted with townspeople who remembered her from before.

"Remember when your mom organized that summer reading program?" Mrs. Snyder asked as Tessa handed her a package of specialty teas. "My Tommy never picked up a book willingly until she got him hooked on those adventure stories. Changed his whole school experience."

"I didn't know that," she admitted.

"Oh yes. She touched so many lives here." Mrs. Snyder patted Tessa's hand. "You have her smile, you know. It's lovely to see you again in Sweet River Falls."

As the woman moved on to the next booth, Tessa realized she had been smiling for hours without having to force it. The tightness that had lived between her shoulder blades for months had loosened slightly. Her hands, which sometimes trembled when she was overwhelmed at the hospital, were steady as she counted change and arranged displays.

"You're a natural at this," Annie commented during a brief lull. "Sure you don't want to trade emergency medicine for small-town retail?"

She laughed, surprising herself with how genuine it sounded. "I don't think my student loans would appreciate the career change."

"Fair enough. But it's nice to see you enjoying yourself."

Was she enjoying herself? She considered the question as she rearranged a display of bookmarks. The constant pressure of the ER, where every decision could mean life or death, was absent here. So was the gnawing anxiety that had plagued her in Denver, the fear that she wasn't good enough or that she would make a catastrophic mistake.

Here, selling books and hot chocolate at a Christmas market, the stakes were beautifully, wonderfully low. No one would die if she recommended the wrong novel. The world wouldn't end if they ran out of peppermint cocoa before noon.

"I guess I am enjoying myself," she admitted. "It's been a while since I did anything just for the joy of it."

Annie nodded, understanding in her eyes. "Sometimes we forget there's more to life than just surviving it."

By noon, Tessa's cheeks hurt from smiling, and

she realized with a start that she was actually enjoying herself. When was the last time that had happened? Here, in the crisp mountain air surrounded by familiar faces and the scent of pine and cinnamon, she felt something unfamiliar stirring inside her. She felt contentment.

"Earth to Tessa," Annie waved a hand in front of her face. "You were a million miles away."

"Sorry," she said, refocusing. "Just taking it all in."

Annie smiled knowingly. "It's different coming back as an adult, isn't it? You see things you missed before."

"I guess I never appreciated how connected everyone is here." Tessa refilled the cookie tray with gingerbread stars.

"That's Sweet River Falls for you. For better or worse, everyone knows everyone."

The afternoon wore on, and Tessa found herself periodically glancing toward the Sweet River Lodge booth. Beckett remained there, working steadily alongside Nora. He seemed to have relaxed somewhat, even smiling occasionally as children admired the intricate wooden ornaments he'd crafted. Once, he looked up and caught Tessa watching him. For a brief moment, their eyes met across the crowded market, and Tessa felt a flutter of something warm and hopeful in her chest.

Then someone stepped between them, breaking the connection, and the moment passed.

Around three o'clock, Annie left to replenish their dwindling stock of hot chocolate, leaving Tessa to mind the booth alone. She was just finishing a sale when she heard her name called.

"Tessa Grant? Is that really you?"

She turned to find herself face-to-face with James Finch, her high school boyfriend. He looked older, of course, with threads of silver at his temples, but his wide, slightly crooked smile was just as she remembered it.

"James," she said, genuinely pleased to see him. "It's been forever."

"Fifteen years, give or take." He leaned against the booth's counter. "Dad told me you were back in town. How long are you staying?"

She shrugged. "Not sure yet. It depends on my father's recovery."

"Well, it's good to see you. You look great."

"Thanks. So do you." She gestured to his left hand, where a wedding band gleamed. "Married life suits you."

He grinned. "Ten years next spring. Two kids, too. They're around here somewhere with my wife, probably loading up on sugar."

"That's wonderful," she said, and meant it. There had been a time when she'd imagined a different future, one where she might have been that wife, and those might have been her children. But that path had closed when she left Sweet River Falls, and she found she had no regrets about it. "You always wanted a family."

"And you always wanted out," James said, but there was no bitterness in his tone. "Did you find what you were looking for in Denver?"

Had she? She'd built a respectable career, had a decent apartment, and colleagues she respected. But friends? Real connections? Those had fallen by the wayside as she threw herself into her work and used exhaustion as a shield against loneliness. "Parts of it. Still working on the rest."

He nodded, understanding in his eyes. "Aren't we all? Well, I'd better go round up the kids. Good seeing you."

After James left, she found herself scanning the market again for Beckett. She spotted him helping a young boy select an ornament, his expression patient and kind as he listened to the child's careful deliberations. The sight made something twist in her chest, a feeling she wasn't quite ready to acknowledge or admit.

Annie returned with fresh supplies, and they worked side by side as the afternoon deepened toward evening. "How are we doing on inventory?" Annie asked, tallying their sales.

She checked their stock. "Almost out of the cinnamon blend, but plenty of everything else."

"Perfect. We're ahead of last year's sales already." Annie beamed, clearly delighted. "Having you here has been a godsend. I usually have to manage this alone."

"I'm happy to help. It's been fun." She was surprised to find she truly meant it.

"Enough fun to stick around through Christmas?" Annie asked, her tone casual but her eyes hopeful.

"I'm not sure. Everything happened so fast with Dad's stroke and me coming back... I haven't had time to think about when I'll return to Denver."

This wasn't entirely true. She'd been thinking about it constantly, especially during those quiet moments when she found herself actually enjoying being back in Sweet River Falls. Her leave from the hospital was open-ended, a fact she'd been careful not to share with her father. Dr. Foster had been clear: "Take all the time you need, Tessa. The ER will still be here when you're ready."

If she was ready.

Annie nodded, not pushing further. "Well, whatever you choose, know that you have people here who care about you."

The simple statement hit her harder than she expected. Did she have people in Denver who truly cared? Colleagues who would notice if she disappeared? Neighbors who would check on her if she didn't show up? The answer made her throat tighten.

"Thank you. That means a lot," she managed.

As the day progressed into early evening, the market took on a magical quality. Christmas lights twinkled against the darkening sky, and the scent of pine and cinnamon filled the air. She found herself caught up in the festive atmosphere, laughing at Annie's stories about past Christmas markets and joining in when a group of carolers passed by their booth. For the first time in longer than she could remember, she felt present, connected to the moment rather than anxiously anticipating the next crisis.

She was arranging a fresh batch of gingerbread cookies when a commotion near the town square caught her attention. A woman's voice rose above the general market noise, high and panicked.

"Mandy? Mandy, where are you? Has anyone seen my daughter?"

Tessa looked up to see a young woman frantically moving between booths, her expression terrified. People were stopping to help, asking questions and looking around.

"What's happening?" Tessa asked Annie, who was already stepping out from behind their booth.

"Sounds like someone's child is missing," Annie said, her face creased with concern. "That's Emily Brown. Her daughter Mandy is about four."

Without hesitation, she followed Annie toward the distraught mother. Years of emergency room training kicked in, focusing her mind and steadying her nerves. This was familiar territory—the ability to stay calm when others couldn't.

"Emily," Annie said as they reached the woman. "What happened? When did you last see Mandy?"

Emily's eyes were wide with fear. "Just a few minutes ago. She was right beside me at the hot chocolate stand, and then I turned to pay, and she was gone. She's wearing a red coat with a white fur hood. Please, she's only four. She's never wandered off before."

"We'll find her," Tessa said firmly, using the same tone she employed with panicking family members in the ER. "She can't have gotten far, and there are plenty of people to help look."

Already, word was spreading through the crowd. Nora Cassidy appeared and leaned close. "You're doing a great job. Go ahead. They'll listen to you."

Tessa nodded, efficiently taking charge. "Everyone, stay calm," she announced in a voice that carried. "We're looking for four-year-old Mandy Brown. She's wearing a red coat. Market vendors, please check under your tables and behind your displays. Parents, keep your children close. Let's spread out and cover the whole square."

As people began spreading out, she felt a presence beside her and turned to find Beckett. The familiar scent of pine and sawdust that always seemed to surround him was oddly comforting in the midst of the growing chaos. His face was set with worry and determination, and his eyes scanned the crowd with focused intensity.

"I'll take the north end," he said quietly, his voice steady and reassuring against the backdrop of worried murmurs and Emily's barely contained sobs.

She nodded, a wave of relief washing through her at his calm approach. Her heart was pounding with a familiar adrenaline rush, but unlike the panic attacks that had plagued her in Denver, this felt purposeful and controlled. "Look for small spaces a child might squeeze into. And check with the vendors selling toys or candy. She might have been attracted to those."

He nodded, his gaze meeting hers for a brief moment before he disappeared into the crowd, his tall figure weaving purposefully through the sea of concerned faces and holiday decorations.

CHAPTER 13

BECKETT WALKED PURPOSEFULLY through the now-anxious crowd. He checked between booths, behind displays, and asked vendors if they'd seen a little girl in a red coat. The minutes ticked by, each one increasing the worry he tried to keep at bay. Children could move quickly, and in a crowded market, there were countless places to hide or become trapped.

He glanced around the crowd and frowned. So many people were searching every inch of the square. What if the girl had wandered off farther? Making an instant decision, he turned and headed between two buildings and out behind them onto the River Walk. There were too many tracks in the snow to know if she'd come this way, but he continued walking along the river.

As he approached a larger area on the River

Walk that had a statue of a pony, he heard a small sound, like a hiccup or a stifled sob. He paused, listening intently, then hurried forward, his heart hammering against his ribs.

There, curled into a tight ball under the pony statue, was a tiny figure in a red coat.

"Mandy?" He kept his voice gentle, fighting to keep the tremor of hope from his words. "Is that you, sweetheart?"

The little girl looked up, her face tear-streaked but unharmed. She nodded mutely, her bottom lip quivering.

"Your mom is looking for you," he said, extending his hand but not moving closer, not wanting to frighten the child further. "She's very worried. Would you like to come out so we can find her?"

She hesitated, then whispered, "I wanted to see the pony, but then it got dark, and I was scared."

"It's okay to be scared. But you're safe now, and your mom really wants to see you." His voice caught on the last words, his throat tight with unexpected emotion.

After a moment's consideration, Mandy crawled forward and took his outstretched hand. He let out a deep breath as his hand closed over hers, warmth flooding through him like sunshine breaking through clouds. The knot in his chest loosened. He scooped the girl into his arms, his muscles relaxing as the weight of worry lifted. Mandy immediately wrapped her small arms around his neck.

"Let's go find your mom." Relief swept through him as he carried her back to the market.

When Emily spotted them walking through the crowd, her cry of joy pierced the winter air, drawing every head in their direction. She rushed forward with outstretched arms, tears streaming down her cheeks.

He carefully transferred Mandy into her mother's desperate embrace, feeling the weight of responsibility lift from his shoulders as the little girl was reunited with her mom. A collective sigh of relief rippled through the market as word spread that the child was found and unharmed. People smiled and nodded at one another, the holiday spirit returning to the festive gathering.

"Thank you," Emily sobbed, her voice breaking as she clutched Mandy against her chest, rocking slightly back and forth. Her fingers trembled as they stroked her daughter's hair. "Thank you so much."

"She went to find the pony. The one on the River Walk." His voice was soft, his heart still racing from the mixture of worry and relief.

"And it got dark and scary, Momma." Mandy's small voice quivered, her eyes still wet with tears but already regaining their childlike brightness.

"Mandy, you know you're not supposed to ever walk away like that." Emily's voice wavered between stern and thankful, her arms never loosening their protective hold.

"So does that mean I don't get the cookie you promised me?" The crowd around them erupted in warm, relieved laughter.

As the drama concluded, he felt a warm hand on his shoulder and turned to find Tessa beside him. "Nice work," she said softly, her voice carrying a note of admiration that made his heart skip a beat.

He shrugged, but a warmth spread through him at her words. "And you did a great job calming everyone down and getting everyone organized to search."

"Years of triage. Keep calm and organize." She shrugged.

Before he could say more, the mayor came up and congratulated him on finding Mandy safe and sound. Nora came over and hugged him. "Good job. Glad you thought to expand the search."

Townsfolk he barely knew hugged him and shook his hand. Tessa stood quietly by his side, watching it all. The market gradually returned to its festive atmosphere.

Tessa looked up at him and grinned. "I'm pretty sure you're the new town hero."

"I just got lucky and looked in the right place."

She laughed. "And you're lousy at taking compliments."

For the first time in days, he didn't immediately

pull away or make an excuse to leave. Instead, they stood together, watching as Emily Brown bought her daughter a cookie, the whole time holding tightly to the little girl's hand.

"It feels good, doesn't it?" she said quietly. "Helping people. Making a difference."

He nodded. "It's why you became a nurse, isn't it?"

"Yes," she admitted. "Though lately, I've been wondering if I've lost sight of that somewhere along the way."

The Christmas lights reflected in her eyes as he looked at her. "Maybe you just needed to come home to remember."

She looked up at him and nodded slowly. "Maybe I did." Then she smiled at him. "Come on, I'm going to buy the town hero a hot chocolate."

She tucked her hand in the crook of his arm, and they wandered slowly through the Christmas market. And hope began to grow in him. The hope that maybe he didn't have to leave. Maybe he could finally find a place to belong. Maybe.

CHAPTER 14

Tessa's hands still tingled with the lingering warmth of Beckett's arm as they walked back to her father's house through the snow-dusted streets of Sweet River Falls. The Christmas market lights twinkled behind them, causing shadows to dance across the pristine white ground. Neither spoke much during their journey home, both lost in thought about the evening's events.

The search for little Mandy had awakened something in Tessa. For the first time in months, she'd felt that rush of purpose, that clarity that used to drive her through grueling ER shifts. Only this time, there hadn't been the crushing weight of responsibility that had eventually broken her.

When they reached the house, her father was already asleep in his recliner, the television playing softly in the background. She gently draped a blanket over him, noting how peaceful he looked. The lines of worry that usually creased his forehead had smoothed out in sleep, making him appear younger.

"Should we wake him?" Beckett whispered.

She shook her head. "Let him rest."

She motioned toward the kitchen, and Beckett followed. The quiet felt different tonight. Not tense or awkward, but thoughtful. As if they were both carefully considering what to say next.

She filled the kettle and set it on the stove. "I think I'll have tea. Want some?"

"Sure." He leaned a hip against the counter.

"You were amazing tonight," she said finally, breaking the silence. "Finding Mandy like that."

He shrugged, his eyes fixed on the floor. "Just did what anyone would do."

"No. Not everyone would have thought to check the River Walk. Not everyone would have known exactly where to look." She turned to face him fully. "You saved that little girl a lot of fear and her mother a lifetime of what-ifs."

He looked up then, and something in his expression made her heart stutter. Vulnerability mixed with a quiet pride that he seemed almost afraid to acknowledge.

"I know what it's like to be lost." He shrugged.

The kettle whistled, and she busied herself with preparing the tea, needing a moment to collect herself. She handed him a steaming mug and nodded toward the back porch. "Want to sit outside? I'll grab a blanket."

They settled into the wooden chairs her father had placed on the small covered porch years ago. She covered them both with the blanket. The snow was falling again, fat flakes drifting lazily from the night sky. The world felt hushed, as if holding its breath.

She cradled her mug between her palms. "You've been avoiding me since that note."

He didn't deny it. He stared out at the snow-covered yard, his profile illuminated by the porch light. "Thought it might be easier. For everyone."

"Easier isn't always better." She took a sip of her tea, letting the warmth spread through her. "I've been doing easier for fifteen years. Running away from this town, from my dad, from anything that might hurt. Look where it got me."

He turned to her then, his eyes searching her face. "Where did it get you?"

"Burned out. Alone. Having panic attacks in supply closets." She gave a humorless laugh. "I was so busy proving I was fine that I didn't notice I was falling apart."

He nodded slowly. "I get that. Prison teaches you to hide any weakness. I got so good at it I almost forgot who I was underneath."

The admission hung between them, delicate as the snowflakes falling beyond the porch roof.

"I'm sorry about that note. People can be cruel."

"People can be scared," he corrected gently. "Fear makes us do ugly things sometimes. Fear of the unknown. Of anything being different than what we're used to. Fear of change."

She understood the fear of change. She was right there, standing on the edge, not knowing which direction to take. Annie's half-attempt to ask her to stay through Christmas and help with the cafe almost looked tempting. But she was a nurse, not a retail clerk or a barista.

She looked at him and sighed. "I'm afraid of change. I just don't know what to do next. Dad and I are starting to work things out, and it seems wrong to leave when we are. But I have a job to get back to in Denver." *Kind of.* "But there's still so much left unsaid between Dad and me."

He set his mug down on the small table beside him. "It was the grief, Tessa. Your dad trying to handle his grief. Grief does strange things to people. Makes them shut down when they should open up." He looked directly at her. "Makes them run when they should stay."

She studied him in the soft light. The strong line of his jaw, the careful way he held himself, as if always aware of the space he occupied. She'd judged him so harshly when she first arrived, assuming the worst based on a label. Now she couldn't imagine the house without him.

"I'm sorry I was so cold when I first got here," she said. "I was wrong about you."

"You were protecting your father. I respect that."

"Still. I should have given you a chance."

He looked at her directly then, his gaze steady. "We're both pretty good at keeping people at a distance, aren't we?"

The observation hit close to home. Too close. She'd built walls so high around herself that sometimes she forgot what it felt like to let anyone in. Her colleagues respected her, but did any of them really know her? When was the last time she'd let herself be vulnerable with another person?

"I think I forgot how to let people in," she admitted. "After Mom died, Dad shut down, and I learned that depending on others just leads to disappointment. So I became self-sufficient. The reliable one. The one who never needed help."

"Until you did." It wasn't a question.

Tessa nodded, feeling the sting of tears. "The panic attacks started about six months ago. Small things at first. Heart racing during a difficult case. Trouble catching my breath in the ambulance bay. Then one day, a patient came in, a car accident victim. Young woman, dark hair like my mom's." She swallowed hard. "I froze. Completely froze.

Had to lock myself in a supply closet until I could breathe again."

He didn't interrupt, didn't try to comfort her with empty platitudes. He just listened, his presence steady and grounding.

She gave a bitter laugh. "Fifteen years of running from my grief, and it finally caught up with me."

"That's the thing about the past. It always finds you eventually," he said softly.

They sat in silence for a moment, watching the snow fall. She felt strangely peaceful, as if sharing her burden had lightened it somehow.

He stretched out his long legs, finally speaking, "I know I withdrew after that note appeared. Old habits. When people look at me like I'm dangerous, it's easier to disappear than to fight it."

"Is that what you're planning to do? Disappear when your program ends next month?"

He didn't answer immediately, and Tessa felt a flutter of anxiety in her chest. The thought of him leaving Sweet River Falls created an unexpected hollow feeling inside her.

"I don't know. I've been taking it one day at a time. That's all I can manage right now," he admitted.

"One small thing," she murmured, remembering their conversation on the River Walk.

He nodded. "One small thing."

A comfortable silence fell between them. The snow continued to fall, transforming the world into something pure and new. She found herself thinking about second chances, about how life sometimes took you on unexpected detours that turned out to be exactly where you needed to go.

"Maybe we can help each other," she said suddenly.

He looked at her, a question in his eyes.

"With the one small thing," she clarified. "Maybe we can be each other's reminders that the past doesn't have to define us. That we're more than our mistakes or our grief."

"I'd like that."

She felt a warmth spreading through her. For the first time in years, perhaps since before her mother died, she felt truly seen by another person. Not as the capable nurse or the estranged daughter, but simply as Tessa, with all her flaws and fears and hopes.

"I'm glad I came home," she said softly. "Even if it took my dad having a stroke to get me here."

"Sometimes we need a wake-up call. Something to shake us out of the patterns we've created."

He was right. Her father's illness had forced her back to Sweet River Falls, but finding Beckett here, understanding him, was changing something fundamental inside her. Making her question the life she'd built in Denver and whether it was truly what she wanted.

He reached over and took her hand in his. "And Tessa, I think your first one small thing should be a conversation with your dad. Talk to him. Really talk. Sort things out."

"That doesn't sound so small to me."

He squeezed her hand. "Maybe not. But it's a good first step."

One small thing at a time. Maybe that was all any of them could do. Face each day, each challenge, each opportunity for connection as it came. And maybe that would be enough. Maybe it would help both of them figure out their future.

CHAPTER 15

Tessa woke before dawn and sat up in bed. She'd spent half the night mentally rehearsing what she needed to say to her father. The words had tumbled through her mind on an endless loop, sometimes clear and purposeful, other times tangled and inadequate.

She slipped out of bed and padded to the window. The snow had stopped sometime during the night, leaving a pristine blanket across the yard. The eastern sky held just a hint of pale light. Another day in Sweet River Falls. Another day of pretending everything was fine.

Except she couldn't pretend anymore.

Beckett's gentle suggestion last night about having an honest conversation with her father had settled deep inside her. One small thing. That's what he'd called it, but it felt enormous. Necessary, but terrifying.

She dressed in jeans and a soft flannel shirt, then headed to the kitchen. To her surprise, her father was already there, sitting at the table with a mug of coffee, staring out the window.

"Morning," she said, her voice sounding unnaturally loud in the quiet kitchen.

Stan turned, his eyes crinkling slightly at the corners. "You're up early."

"Couldn't sleep. Where's Beckett?" She poured herself coffee, wrapping her hands around the warm mug.

"Garage. Said he wanted to finish that bookshelf he's been working on."

She nodded, taking a careful sip of her coffee. Perfect timing. Or maybe Beckett had sensed what was coming.

She took a deep breath. "Dad, can we talk?"

Something in her tone must have alerted him because his expression shifted, and a wariness entered his eyes. "About what?"

"About... us. About after Mom died."

Stan's fingers tightened around his mug. He looked away, back toward the window. "What's there to talk about? It was a long time ago."

She pulled out a chair and sat across from him. "But it wasn't just then, was it? It's been our entire relationship since. We need to talk about why you pushed me so hard."

Her father's jaw tightened. For a moment, she thought he might get up and leave the room, the way he used to whenever conversations veered toward anything emotional. But he stayed, though his gaze remained fixed on the yard outside.

"What do you mean, pushed you?"

Tessa forced herself to keep her voice steady. "Dad. The constant expectations. The way nothing was ever good enough. Straight As weren't enough. Being top of my class wasn't enough. Being a nurse wasn't enough. It always had to be more."

He shook his head slightly. "I wanted you to succeed."

"No." The word came out sharper than she intended. "It wasn't about success. It was about control."

Her father's eyes snapped to hers, a flash of something—Anger? Recognition?—crossing his face before his expression went neutral.

"After Mom died, everything changed. You changed. It was like... like you couldn't handle the grief, so you channeled everything into making sure I was perfect."

His fingers drummed against the table, a nervous habit she'd forgotten about until this moment. "You don't understand."

"Then help me understand. Because I've spent

fifteen years trying to figure it out on my own, and all I know is that I left here because I couldn't breathe anymore. Because nothing I did was ever enough for you."

A long silence stretched between them. Outside, the sky had lightened to a pale blue, as sunlight began to glint off the snow. From somewhere distant, she could hear the rhythmic sound of Beckett's sanding in the garage.

Finally, he set down his mug with a heavy sigh. "I didn't know what else to do."

The simple admission hung in the air between them.

"After your mother died," he continued, his voice rougher than usual, "I was... lost. She was always the one who knew what to do and how to parent. How to love openly." He swallowed hard. "All I knew was that the world was suddenly terrifying. That I could lose everything in an instant."

She stayed silent, afraid that if she spoke, he might retreat back into himself.

"I couldn't control what happened to your mother. The cancer, the treatments that didn't work, any of it." His eyes, when they met hers, held a vulnerability she'd never seen before. "But I thought maybe I could control what happened to you. If you were prepared, if you were strong enough, smart enough, capable enough... maybe life wouldn't hurt you the way it hurt her. The way losing her hurt me."

The revelation settled over her like a physical weight. All these years, she'd thought his pushing came from disappointment, from her not measuring up. But it had been fear. Raw, unprocessed fear.

"Dad," she said softly, "you can't protect people from life."

"I know that now. But back then, it was all I had. If I pushed you to excel, to be independent and strong, then maybe you'd be okay if something happened to me too."

"But you pushed me away instead."

He nodded, a small, pained movement. "I didn't know how to do both. Didn't know how to love you the way she would have and prepare you for a world that takes people too soon. So I focused on making you strong. And I lost sight of everything else."

She felt a knot form in her throat. "I needed my dad. Not a drill sergeant."

"I know." His voice cracked slightly. "By the time I realized what was happening between us, you were already pulling away. And then you were gone."

The kitchen fell silent again, the enormity of fifteen years of misunderstanding hanging between them. She thought of all the holidays spent alone, the graduations where she'd scanned the audience hoping to see his face, and the nights in her apartment when she'd almost called but then set the phone down.

"I thought you were disappointed in me. That I wasn't living up to some standard you had," she finally said.

He shook his head, looking genuinely surprised. "Disappointed? Tessa, I've always been proud of you. Maybe too proud. You were so much like your mother. So smart and determined. I just wanted to make sure you had the strength I didn't have when we lost her."

"But you made me feel like nothing I did was ever enough."

"Because I was terrified." His admission came quietly. "Every time you achieved something, I thought, 'This is good, but will it be enough to protect her?' And the answer was always no, because nothing can really protect us from loss."

She felt tears prick at her eyes. "So instead of dealing with your grief, you put all that fear on me."

He looked away, shame evident in the slump of his shoulders. "I didn't know how else to be. Your mother was always the heart of this family. Without her, I just... defaulted to what I knew. Structure. Discipline. Push forward and don't look back."

"It drove us apart."

"Yes." The simple acknowledgment seemed to deflate him further. "And by the time I realized what I'd done, you were gone, building your life in Denver without me."

She thought about her life in Denver—the long shifts at the hospital, the apartment she barely spent time in, the colleagues she never quite connected with beyond work. Had she really built a life there? Or had she just been running, still trying to prove herself worthy of... something?

"I've been on medical leave," she admitted. The words felt strange to say out loud. "That's why I could come home when Fran told me what happened to you. I'm not... I'm not handling things well at work."

Her father's brow creased with concern. "What happened?"

"Panic attacks." Saying it aloud still made her feel ashamed, as if admitting weakness. "I was in the middle of a trauma case and suddenly couldn't breathe. Couldn't think. Had to lock myself in a supply closet until it passed."

"Oh, Tessa." The genuine concern in his voice made her throat tighten again.

"It wasn't the first time. Just the worst." She stared down at her coffee, now gone cold. "I've been pushing myself so hard for so long, trying to be perfect, trying to prove... I don't even know what anymore. And it all just crashed down."

He reached across the table, hesitating before gently placing his hand over hers. The gesture was so unexpected, so unlike him, that she had to blink back tears.

"I did that to you," he said quietly. "Made you think you had to be perfect."

She turned her hand to grasp his. "We both did it. I internalized it. Kept pushing myself even when you weren't there to push me anymore."

They sat in silence for a moment. Outside, the morning had fully arrived, and sunlight streamed through the window.

"I don't know how to fix this," he finally said.

"I don't either." She offered a small, sad smile. "But maybe acknowledging it is a start."

Her father nodded, squeezing her hand before releasing it. "For what it's worth, I am proud of you. Not because of what you've accomplished, but because of who you are. I should have told you that more."

"You never told me at all," she said, but without the bitterness that would have colored the words even a few weeks ago.

"I know." He looked genuinely regretful. "After your mother died, I thought showing emotion was a weakness. That if I let myself feel anything, I'd fall apart completely."

"And now?"

He gestured vaguely around the kitchen. "Now I'm learning. Slowly. Having Beckett here... it's been good. He's teaching an old dog new tricks, I suppose."

She thought about Beckett, out in the garage giving them space for this conversation. How he seemed to understand both of them, despite knowing them for such different lengths of time.

"He's good at seeing people," she said. "Really seeing them."

He nodded. "That he is." He looked at her curiously. "You two seem to be getting along better."

"We are. He's helped me see things differently." She wasn't ready to examine the feeling that spread through her at the thought of Beckett.

"Me too." He cleared his throat. "Listen, Tessa. I know I can't make up for all those years, but I'd like to try to do better, if you'll let me."

The sincerity in his voice made her heart ache. "I'd like that too."

"And maybe," he added hesitantly, "you could stay a little longer? Not just because of my health, but because... well, it's Christmas soon. And it would be nice to have you home."

Home. The word hung in the air.

"I'll think about it," she said, not ready to commit but not wanting to refuse outright either.

He nodded, accepting her answer. "That's fair." He stood up, refilling his coffee mug. "I should probably check on Beckett, make sure he's not freezing out there."

Tessa watched him move toward the door, noting how much older he looked than when she'd left fifteen years ago. How much more vulnerable.

"Dad," she called after him. He turned, eyebrows raised in question. "Thank you for talking about this."

He gave a small nod, his eyes softer than she'd seen them in years. "Thank you for asking."

After he left, Tessa remained at the table, letting the conversation settle around her. It wasn't a perfect resolution. There were still years of hurt and misunderstanding between them. But it felt like a beginning, a clearing of old ground where something new might eventually grow.

She thought about what Beckett had said last night about taking life one small thing at a time. This conversation had been her small thing, and somehow, facing it had made the next steps seem a little less daunting.

Tessa stood and walked to the window, watching as her father crossed the yard to the garage. She could see Beckett through the open door, looking up as Stan approached, his expression shifting from concentration to welcome. The two men spoke briefly, then Beckett handed her father a piece of sandpaper, making room for him at the workbench.

The sight stirred something inside her—a recognition of how much had changed while she was gone, but also how much opportunity there might be in those changes. Her father was different now. She was different too. And maybe that meant they could find a new way forward together.

One small thing at a time, she reminded herself. Today, it had been an honest conversation with her father. Tomorrow, it might be something else entirely. But for the first time in longer than she could remember, the future didn't feel like a burden she had to perfectly prepare for. Instead, it felt like a path with multiple possibilities, none of them requiring perfection.

She glanced out the window one more time. Her father and Beckett were working side by side now, the morning sun illuminating them in the open garage door. Two men at different stages of life, both carrying their own burdens, both finding some measure of peace in simple, productive work.

She smiled to herself. Perhaps there was something to learn there too. About healing. About second chances. About home.

She looked out the window once more. The morning was bright and sparkled off the icicles hanging from the eaves. And somewhere in the yard between the house and garage, in the space between her past and her uncertain future, she thought she might find her next small step forward.

CHAPTER 16

Tessa slipped on her boots and glanced through the window at the bright sunshine reflecting off the snow. After her emotional conversation with her father that morning, she needed some air.

She scribbled a quick note on the pad by the phone: "Gone for a walk. Back soon." Her father was napping, and Beckett had disappeared to the garage after lunch.

Grabbing her coat from the hook by the door, she stepped outside, inhaling deeply as the cold air filled her lungs. She hadn't planned where to go, but her feet naturally turned toward town and the River Walk. The path had been cleared of snow, making it one of the few places she could walk without trudging through knee-deep drifts.

The River Walk was quiet this afternoon. Most people were probably at work or staying indoors where it was warm. She welcomed the solitude. She needed time to process everything her father had said.

"I was trying to make you strong enough to survive in a world that hurt us both." His words echoed in her mind as she walked alongside the rushing water of the Sweet River. All those years, she'd interpreted his pushing as disappointment when really, it had been fear.

Fear of losing her too.

She paused at a wooden bench overlooking the water and brushed off the light dusting of snow before sitting down. The river was partially frozen along the edges, but the center still flowed, dark and swift against the white landscape. Like life, she thought. No matter how much things freeze and seem to stop, underneath, everything keeps moving forward.

She'd spent fifteen years running from this place, convinced her father didn't want her and didn't care. And all that time, he'd been keeping her graduation photo beside his bed, saving every card she sent, and speaking proudly of her to anyone who would listen.

Her throat tightened. So much time they'd wasted. So many holidays and ordinary days they could have shared.

The sound of footsteps pulled her from her thoughts. She turned to see Beckett approaching, his tall figure bundled against the cold, his breath visible in the crisp air.

He stopped a few feet away. "Hey. Mind if I join you?"

She shook her head and moved over on the bench, making room for him.

"I saw your note and figured this is where you'd head." He sat beside her, leaving a respectful distance between them. "And Stan mentioned you two had a good talk this morning. Thought I'd check on you. Make sure you're okay."

"He said that?" She glanced at him, surprised.

Beckett nodded, his eyes studying her face. "He said he thought you'd worked some things out. Seemed hopeful."

"Hopeful," she repeated softly. The word felt strange and wonderful at the same time. When was the last time she'd associated hope with her relationship with her father?

She turned toward the river again, watching the water flow beneath patches of ice. The tears she'd been holding back welled up suddenly, spilling onto her cheeks before she could stop them.

"Tessa?" Beckett's voice was gentle with concern. "What's wrong?"

She pulled off her glove and swiped at her face. "I've been so wrong about him. All these years." Her voice caught. "I shouldn't have left for so long. I should have tried to talk to him before all this time went by."

"You were hurt. We all do what we need to survive when we're hurting."

"But fifteen years, Beckett." She shook her head. "Fifteen years of barely speaking to my father. Coming home only when I absolutely had to. And now..." She motioned helplessly. "Now I find out he's been proud of me all along. That he was just scared and didn't know how to show it."

He didn't offer empty reassurances or tell her not to cry. He just sat with her, present and steady as she worked through her emotions.

"Thank you," she said after a moment. "For suggesting I talk to him. I don't think I would have had the courage otherwise."

"You would have. Maybe not today or tomorrow, but you would have found your way there eventually. You're stronger than you give yourself credit for."

She smiled through her tears. "That's the nicest thing anyone's said to me in a long time."

They sat in comfortable silence, watching the river together. The sun was beginning its early winter descent, casting shadows across the snow.

She finally looked at him and smiled. "So what about you? You told me to talk to my dad as my first small thing. What will yours be?"

He looked thoughtful and tugged at the zipper

of his jacket. "I'm not sure yet. There are a lot of things I could work on."

"Like what?"

He shrugged. "Learning to trust people again. Not assuming everyone's going to judge me for my past. Actually believing I deserve a second chance."

His honesty touched her. In the short time she'd known him, Beckett had shown more genuine self-awareness than most people she'd met in her entire life.

"For what it's worth, I think you're doing pretty well already."

A small smile lifted the corner of his mouth. "Thanks."

The sound of footsteps on the path drew their attention. A man was approaching from the direction of town, wearing expensive boots and a heavy wool coat. As he drew closer, Tessa recognized Walter Dobbs, the businessman who'd tried to develop condos around Lone Elk Lake, and the man Annie thought might have posted the note about Beckett.

Dobbs slowed as he spotted them, his expression hardening when his gaze fell on Beckett. It was clear from his body language that he was considering turning around to avoid them.

Before he could, Beckett stood and stepped forward, holding out his hand. "Mr. Dobbs."

Dobbs hesitated, eyeing Beckett's extended hand with obvious reluctance.

"I don't think we've been formally introduced," Beckett continued, his voice calm and steady. "I'm Beckett. I've been living with Stan Grant for a while."

"I know who you are," Dobbs said stiffly, making no move to take Beckett's hand.

She felt a surge of protectiveness. She started to stand, ready to intervene, but something in Beckett's posture stopped her. He wasn't backing down, but there was no aggression in his stance either.

"I wanted to thank you for the donation you made to the children's reading program at Bookish Cafe," Beckett said. "Annie mentioned it helped them buy a lot of new books for the kids."

Surprise flickered across Dobbs's face. Whatever he'd been expecting Beckett to say, it wasn't that.

"The program needed funding, and it's a tax write-off to me," he said after a moment.

"Well, it made a difference," Beckett said. "I help out with the reading sessions sometimes. The kids really enjoy the new books."

Dobbs gave a short nod, then, after a brief hesitation, reached out and briefly shook Beckett's hand. "Good to know." He glanced at Tessa. "Ms. Grant. Good to see you back in town."

"Thank you, Mr. Dobbs."

With another nod, Dobbs continued on his way.

When he was out of earshot, Beckett turned to her and grinned, a genuine smile that transformed his usually serious face. "That's my first small thing."

She couldn't help but laugh. "You planned that?"

"Not exactly. But when I saw him coming, I figured it was as good a time as any to start somewhere." He sat back down beside her. "I'm pretty sure he's the one who left that note at the cafe."

"That's what Annie thought too." She shook her head in disbelief. "And you just thanked him for a donation? I would have called him out."

"What good would that do? He already thinks the worst of me. Confronting him would only confirm what he believes. Sometimes the best way to change someone's mind is to show them they're wrong, not tell them."

She studied him, impressed by his wisdom and restraint. "That's... remarkably mature."

"That's me." He grinned. "Just a remarkably mature man. Everyone says that about me."

She laughed. "As they should." The sun was sinking lower, and the temperature dropping with it. She shivered slightly.

"We should head back," he said, noticing. "It'll be dark soon."

They stood and brushed snow from their clothes. As they began walking back toward town, she found herself moving closer to Beckett, their arms occasionally brushing. Neither of them moved away.

"Have you decided if you'll stay?" she asked after they'd walked in comfortable silence for a while. "After your program ends next month?"

"I don't know. There's work here I enjoy. People who've been kind." He glanced at her. "But there are also people like Dobbs who'll never see past what I did."

"There are people like that everywhere," she pointed out. "At least here, you have people who know the real you."

"What about you?" he asked. "Will you go back to Denver?"

The question hung between them, suddenly weighted with more significance than a simple inquiry about her plans.

"I don't know either," she admitted. "I need to figure out what I want to do about my job. And now with my dad…" She trailed off. "I've been thinking maybe I could stay through Christmas… and maybe longer."

Something like hope flickered across his face. "I'm sure Stan would like that."

"Just Stan?" she asked, feeling suddenly brave.

He stopped walking and turned to face her. In the fading light, his eyes were serious and intent. "No," he said quietly. "Not just Stan."

Her heartbeat quickened. They stood there, their breath visible in the cold air between them. For a moment, she thought he might kiss her. Part of her wanted him to.

Instead, he gently tucked a strand of hair behind her ear, his gloved hand lingering briefly against her cheek. "We should get back," he said, his voice low. "Your dad will be wondering where we are."

She nodded, unable to speak past the sudden tightness in her throat. As they resumed walking, his hand found hers, warm even through their gloves. This small gesture felt like another first step toward something neither of them was ready to put a name to.

One small thing at a time, she thought. Today, she'd begun to heal her relationship with her father. She'd allowed herself to feel something other than anxiety and exhaustion.

And maybe, she'd found a reason to stay in Sweet River Falls a little longer.

CHAPTER 17

THE NEXT MORNING, Tessa woke to the sound of her father moving around in the kitchen earlier than usual. She could hear him humming under his breath, something she hadn't heard since she was a child. The melody was familiar but distant, like a half-remembered dream.

She quickly got dressed, headed to the kitchen, and found her father already dressed and drinking coffee at the kitchen table. His eyes held a brightness she hadn't seen since her arrival, and he looked up at her with something that resembled excitement.

"Good morning, sweetheart," he said, the endearment falling easily from his lips. "I hope you don't have any big plans today."

She poured herself coffee, still adjusting to this version of her father who used pet names and made plans. "Nothing specific. Why?"

"We're going to get a Christmas tree today. All three of us. I haven't bought my daughter a tree in years, and it's high time I did." Her father's voice carried a determination that said he would accept no argument.

She hadn't had a Christmas tree since her mom died. Her dad never wanted to put one up. Then she moved to Denver, and her small apartment had never seemed to warrant the effort, and working holiday shifts at the hospital had made it easy to skip the traditions that reminded her of what she'd lost.

"Dad, you don't have to—"

"I want to," he interrupted firmly. "Your mother loved Christmas trees. She'd spend hours getting the lights just right, making sure every ornament had its perfect spot." His voice softened with memory. "She'd want us to have a tree."

Beckett appeared in the doorway. "Morning," he said quietly, glancing between them as if sensing the emotional undercurrent.

Her father stood with more energy than she had seen from him since his stroke. "Perfect timing. Go get your coat, Beckett. We're going tree shopping."

"Stan, you sure you're up for this?" Beckett asked, concern evident in his voice.

"I'm sure." Her father's tone left no room for debate. "Doctor said I need to stay active, didn't he? Besides, it's about time we acted like a family around here."

Her throat tightened at hearing the word family. She watched her father bustle around the kitchen, cleaning up his breakfast dishes with purposeful movements. This was the man she remembered from before her mother's death, the one who had made pancakes on Saturday mornings and helped her build snowmen in the backyard.

Twenty minutes later, they were driving through town in Beckett's truck. The tree lot was set up in the parking lot behind the hardware store. The lot was strung with colorful lights and filled with the sharp, clean scent of pine.

"Now, we need a good one," her father announced as they walked among the rows of trees. "None of these scraggly things. Your mother always said a Christmas tree should be full enough to hide a few imperfections but not so perfect it looked fake."

She found herself smiling at the memory. Her mother had indeed been particular about their Christmas tree, walking the entire lot twice before making her selection. She watched her father examine a Douglas fir with the same careful atten- tion her mother used to show.

"What about this one?" Beckett called from a few rows over. He stood next to a tree that was tall enough to fit in their living room but not so large it would overwhelm the space. Its branches were full and even, with a perfect triangular shape.

Her father walked over and circled the tree slowly, nodding his approval. "That's a beauty. Good eye, Beckett." He looked at Tessa. "What do you think, sweetheart?"

The endearment still caught her off guard, but she was beginning to welcome it. "It's perfect," she said, and meant it.

While Beckett and the lot owner secured the tree to the truck, her father pulled Tessa aside. "I know this might seem sudden," he said, his breath forming small clouds in the cold air. "But I've been thinking about what we talked about yesterday. About all the years we lost."

"Dad—"

"Let me finish," he said gently. "I don't want to waste any more time being afraid. Your mother would be furious with both of us for letting Christmas pass by without a tree. I'm surprised she hasn't haunted the house until we got our act together."

She laughed despite the tears threatening at the corners of her eyes. "I'm surprised she hasn't either."

"So we're going to do this right. Tree, decorations, the whole thing. Like we used to."

The drive home was filled with Stan's stories about past Christmases, memories Tessa had pushed away because they hurt too much to remember. But now, sitting in the warm cab of the truck with the scent of pine filling the air, she found herself adding her own memories to his stories.

Back at the house, setting up the tree proved to be more complicated than any of them had anticipated. The tree stand was ancient and temperamental, and it took all three of them working together to get the tree straight and stable.

"Little more to the left," her father directed from his spot on the couch, where she had insisted he supervise rather than crawl around on the floor. "No, too much. Back the other way."

She and Beckett exchanged amused glances as they adjusted the tree for the fifth time. She was struck by how natural this felt, the three of them working together toward a common goal. When had she last felt part of something like this?

"There," her father said finally. "Perfect."

They stepped back to admire their work. The tree stood in the corner of the living room where her mother had always placed it, near the window so the lights would be visible from outside. Even without decorations, it transformed the room, making it feel more like home than it had since her arrival.

"We need to get the decorations down from the attic," her father said. "You two will have to brave the spiders up there."

"I can handle spiders," she said, surprising herself. A week ago, she would have been planning her escape route back to Denver. Now she was volunteering to decorate Christmas trees and face attic spiders.

"Good." Her father reached into his pocket and pulled out a small wrapped box. "But first, I have something for you."

She stared at the box, wrapped in paper that was clearly older than this Christmas season. The tape was yellowed, and the bow was slightly crushed, as if it had been waiting for the right moment for quite some time.

"Dad, what is this?"

"Open it." He nodded at the box.

With trembling fingers, she unwrapped the small box. Inside, nestled in faded tissue paper, was her mother's locket. The gold heart was just as she remembered it, delicate and beautiful, with tiny flowers engraved around the edges.

"Oh," she breathed, lifting it from the box. The chain was fine and elegant, and when she opened the locket, she found her parents' wedding photo inside, just as it had always been.

"She'd want you to have it now. I should have given it to you years ago, but I..." He paused, searching for words. "I guess I wasn't ready to let go of another piece of her."

Tears blurred her vision as she held the locket. "Dad, I can't take this. It's yours."

"No, sweetheart. It's yours. It was always meant

to be yours." He stood up from the couch and walked over to her. "Your mother wore that every day of our marriage. She used to say it held all the love in our family, and that someday she'd pass it on to you so you could fill it with your own love."

Her hands shook as she fastened the chain around her neck. The locket felt warm against her skin, as if it still held some of her mother's presence. "Thank you," she whispered.

Her father pulled her into a hug, and for a moment they stood there holding each other beside their Christmas tree, fifteen years of hurt and misunderstanding beginning to heal in that simple embrace.

When they separated, her father turned to Beckett, who had been quietly observing from near the doorway, giving them space for their private moment.

"Beckett," her father said, his voice carrying a gravity that made both Tessa and Beckett pay attention. "I need to say something to you too."

Beckett straightened, wariness flickering across his features. "Stan, you don't need to—"

"Yes, I do. I need to thank you for being there when I needed help. When I was too stubborn and scared to ask my own daughter to come home, you showed up. You've been taking care of me, taking care of this house, and taking care of things I couldn't manage on my own."

She watched the exchange, seeing how uncomfortable Beckett was with the praise, how he seemed to shrink away from acknowledgment of his kindness.

"You didn't just help me with daily tasks. You helped me remember how to be part of something bigger than my own grief and fear. You showed me that people can change, that second chances matter, and that family isn't always about blood."

Beckett's jaw worked silently, emotion clearly struggling beneath his composed exterior.

"So thank you. For everything. For being the son I needed when I was too proud to admit I needed anyone."

The words hung in the air, heavy with meaning. She felt her heart clench at the sight of Beckett's carefully controlled expression, the way he was trying so hard not to let the emotion show.

"Thank you, Stan," Beckett said finally, his voice rough. "That means more than you know."

Her father nodded and turned back to Tessa. "And you," he said, his eyes bright with unshed tears. "I'm proud of the woman you've become. So proud. I'm sorry for how I tried to shape you with fear instead of love. Your mother would have done it better."

"Dad—"

"She would have helped you find your strength without making you feel like you had to be strong all the time. She would have let you be scared some-times, let you make mistakes without feeling like the world would end." His voice broke slightly. "I failed you in that way, and I'm sorry."

She felt the locket warm against her chest, and for a moment, she could almost feel her mother's presence in the room with them, approving of this moment of honesty and love.

"I'm staying through Christmas," she said suddenly, the words coming from somewhere deep inside her. "Maybe longer."

The smile that spread across her father's face was like the sunrise after a long night. It trans-formed his entire face, erasing years of worry and sadness in an instant.

"Best medicine a man could have," he said, his voice full of joy.

As Tessa looked around the room at the three of them standing beside their Christmas tree, she felt something she hadn't experienced in years. She felt the sense of being exactly where she belonged.

She was looking forward to making new memo-ries that could coexist with the old ones. She was looking forward to Christmas morning, to whatever came after, and taking life one small thing at a time with these two men who had somehow become her family.

CHAPTER 18

TESSA WOKE on Christmas Eve morning to sunlight streaming through her childhood bedroom window and the sound of her father's voice drifting from the kitchen. She stretched, feeling more rested than she had in months. The house smelled like coffee and something sweet—cinnamon rolls, maybe. Miss Judy had dropped off a batch yesterday evening along with a casserole for their Christmas Eve dinner.

She padded into the kitchen in her flannel pajamas and fuzzy slippers, expecting to find both men at the kitchen table with their usual morning coffee ritual. Instead, she found only her father, sitting with his newspaper spread before him and a steaming mug in his hands.

"Morning, sweetheart." He looked up with a

smile that still caught her off guard with its warmth. "Sleep well?"

"I did." She poured herself coffee from the pot, noting it was still nearly full. "Where's Beckett?"

"Left early this morning. Said he had something to take care of for Nora at the lodge." He folded his paper and set it aside. "He'll be back later."

She nodded, trying to ignore the small flutter of disappointment in her chest. Over the past days, she'd grown accustomed to their three-way breakfast conversations and the easy rhythm they'd developed as a makeshift family. Beckett's quiet presence had become something she looked forward to, something that anchored her mornings in a way she hadn't expected.

"Big day today," her father said, watching her over the rim of his mug. "Christmas Eve candlelight walk through town. You remember those, don't you?"

"Vaguely." She settled into the chair across from him. "I think I was pretty young the last time we went."

Pain flickered across his features, but he pushed through it. "Your mother loved the candlelight walk. Said it made the whole town look like something out of a fairy tale." He cleared his throat. "I thought maybe this year we could go again. All three of us."

"I'd like that."

Her father's smile could have powered the Christmas lights on Main Street.

They spent the morning in comfortable companionship, her father reading aloud bits from the local paper while they both ate Miss Judy's cinnamon rolls. She'd forgotten how peaceful mornings could be when they weren't punctuated by hospital pages and emergency calls. Here, the biggest crisis was whether they had enough milk for the pancakes.

Around noon, she decided to take a walk to clear her head and maybe stop by the Bookish Cafe to see if Annie needed help with any last-minute Christmas preparations. She bundled up in her coat and boots and left a note for her father, who was dozing in his recliner with a book open on his chest.

The air was crisp and clean, with the promise of snow in the heavy gray clouds gathering over the mountains. Main Street buzzed with last-minute shoppers and families preparing for the evening's festivities. She found herself smiling at the familiar faces, returning waves from people who remembered her as a girl.

When she returned home an hour later, she found a small package sitting on the front porch. Her name was written across the brown paper wrapping in careful, precise handwriting she recognized as Beckett's. Her heart did something complicated in her chest as she picked it up.

Inside the house, she settled on the couch and carefully unwrapped the package. Nestled in tissue paper was a small wooden ornament carved with exquisite detail. It was shaped like a stethoscope, but where the chest piece would normally be, Beckett had carved a perfect heart. The wood was smooth and warm in her hands, polished to a soft sheen that caught the light.

A folded piece of paper fell from the tissue. She picked it up and opened it.

For the healer who doesn't know she's the one who needed healing most.

She stared at the words until they blurred, her throat tight with emotion. The ornament was beautiful, but it was the message that undid her completely. In one simple sentence, Beckett had captured something she'd been too afraid to acknowledge—that coming home hadn't just been about caring for her father. It had been about finding the pieces of herself she'd lost along the way.

She was still sitting there, turning the ornament over in her hands when she heard Beckett's truck pull into the driveway. Her pulse quickened as his footsteps approached the front door.

"Tessa?" He appeared in the doorway, snow dusting his dark jacket. His eyes went immediately to the ornament in her hands, and a flush crept up his neck. "You found it."

"It's beautiful." The words came out softer than she'd intended. "Beckett, I don't know what to say."

He shifted his weight, suddenly looking uncertain. "If it's too much, I understand. I just thought—"

"It's perfect." She stood, crossing to where he stood in the doorway. "Thank you. For this, and for seeing me. Really seeing me."

Something shifted in his expression, the wariness giving way to something warmer. "You make it easy."

They stood there for a moment, the air between them charged with unspoken possibilities. Then her father's voice called from the kitchen, asking if Beckett was back, and the spell broke.

"I should help him with lunch," Beckett said, but his eyes lingered on her face.

"He's been napping. He had a cinnamon roll for breakfast, but I think Miss Judy's cinnamon rolls have been calling his name again, and he'll want one for lunch."

Beckett's laugh was soft and genuine. "Me too, if I'm being honest."

The afternoon passed in a blur of preparation and anticipation. She helped her father choose his warmest coat and scarf for the evening's festivities, while Beckett made sure they had working flashlights in case the candles blew out. It felt like preparing for a family outing, something she hadn't experienced in so long she'd forgotten what it felt like to belong to something bigger than herself.

As evening approached, snow began to fall in earnest, fat flakes that clung to the windows and transformed the familiar landscape into something magical. She stood at the living room window, watching the world turn white, when Beckett appeared beside her.

"Second thoughts?" he asked quietly.

"No." She was surprised to realize it was true. "I'm actually looking forward to it."

"Your dad's been talking about it all week. I think it means a lot to him, having you here, and going on the Christmas walk with him."

"What about you?" The question slipped out before she could stop it. "Does it mean something to you?"

He was quiet for so long she thought he might not answer. When he finally spoke, his voice was barely above a whisper.

"Everything."

The word hung in the air between them, heavy with implication. She felt her cheeks warm, but she didn't look away from his steady gaze.

"Ready to go?" Her dad appeared in the doorway, wrapped in his heavy winter coat and looking more excited than she'd seen him in years. "Don't want to miss any of it."

The walk to Main Street was magical. Snow

continued to fall, muffling their footsteps and coating the world in pristine white. Other families moved along the sidewalks with them, all heading toward the warm glow of lights that marked the town's Christmas celebration.

Main Street had been transformed. Luminarias lined the sidewalks, their soft light flickering through the falling snow. The shop windows glowed with warm light and holiday displays. At the center of it all stood the town Christmas tree.

"Oh," she breathed, stopping in her tracks. "It's beautiful."

"This town knows how to do Christmas right," her dad said, pride evident in his voice.

They joined the crowd gathering around the tree, accepting candles from volunteers who moved through the group with lighters. She found herself between her father and Beckett, their shoulders touching as they huddled together against the cold.

Pastor Williams stepped forward to offer a brief blessing, his words carrying clearly through the still night air. He spoke of hope and healing, of second chances and the power of coming home. She felt the words settle into her heart.

As the crowd began to move in a slow procession down Main Street, candles flickering like earthbound stars, she caught sight of a familiar figure approaching through the crowd.

"Dr. Miller," her father called out, raising his free hand in greeting.

The doctor made his way over to them, his own candle shining warm light on his weathered features. "Stan, good to see you out and about. And Tessa, hello."

"Hello, Dr. Miller." She shifted her candle to her left hand, extending her right for a handshake.

"I heard about how you handled things at the Christmas market last week," Dr. Miller said, his handshake firm and warm. "Quick thinking, excellent organizational skills. That little girl's parents can't stop talking about how calm and competent you were in a crisis."

She felt heat rise in her cheeks. "I just did what anyone would do."

Dr. Miller shook his head. "No, you did what a good nurse would do. Your father tells me you work in emergency medicine in Denver?"

"I did." The correction slipped out before she could stop it. "I'm currently on leave."

"Ah." Something knowing flickered in the doctor's eyes. "Well, if you ever decide you've had enough of the big city pace, I'd love to have you consider our little clinic here in Sweet River Falls. We could use someone with your skills and temperament."

She stared at him, speechless, as the implications sank in. A job here. A reason to stay. A chance to practice medicine without the crushing pressure that had nearly broken her.

"I..." she started, then stopped. "I don't know what to say."

"Say you'll think about it," Dr. Miller said with a kind smile. "No pressure, but the offer stands. Small-town medicine is different. Slower pace, but no less meaningful. Sometimes more so."

He moved on to greet other members of the procession, leaving her reeling. Beside her, she felt Beckett's questioning gaze, but she couldn't look at him. Not yet. The possibility Dr. Miller had just laid before her was too big, too overwhelming to process with an audience.

The procession continued down Main Street, past the glowing shop windows and through the gentle snowfall. She moved as if in a dream, her mind spinning with possibilities she'd never allowed herself to consider. Stay in Sweet River Falls. Work at the clinic. Build a life here, in the town where she'd grown up, surrounded by people who knew her story and cared about her anyway.

As they reached the end of Main Street and began the slow turn back toward the town square, church bells began to ring out across the valley. The sound was clear and sweet, cutting through the snow-muffled night like a promise. She looked up at the bell tower, then at her father's face, glowing with contentment in the candlelight. Finally, she let herself look at Beckett.

He was watching her with an expression she couldn't quite read. Hope, maybe. Or fear. Perhaps both.

The crowd gathered once more around the Christmas tree as the bells continued to ring. Someone began singing "Silent Night," and other voices joined in, creating a harmony that seemed to rise with the falling snow. She added her own voice to the chorus, the familiar words coming back to her from childhood memories of Christmas services with her mother.

As the last notes faded away, the crowd remained quiet for a moment, then they broke into applause. People shouted Merry Christmas, children laughed, and Tessa felt something inside her chest expand and settle at the same time.

She stood between her father and Beckett, warm candlelight flickering in her hands and warmth spreading through her heart. She'd come home to care for someone else, but somewhere along the way, she'd found her own healing. In the quiet strength of the man beside her, in the tentative rebuilding of her relationship with her father, and in the embrace of a community that remembered her as a child and welcomed her back as an adult.

The snow continued to fall, blessing the town and its people with the promise of new beginnings.

She closed her eyes and let herself feel it all—the cold air on her face, the warmth of the candle in her hands, the solid presence of the two men who had somehow become her anchors in a world where she had felt unmoored for so long.

When she opened her eyes again, Beckett was watching her. In the flickering light of a hundred candles, she saw her own hope reflected back at her.

The bells continued to ring out across Sweet River Falls, carrying their message of peace and possibility into the snowy night. And then she knew for certain, Tessa Grant was exactly where she belonged.

CHAPTER 19

THEY RETURNED HOME from the candlelight walk with snow still clinging to their coats and the warmth of community celebration glowing in their faces. Her father headed straight for his favorite chair by the fireplace, settling in with a contented sigh as Beckett knelt to build up the fire. The flames caught and danced, casting golden light across the living room and the Christmas tree they'd decorated together just days before.

She stood in the doorway for a moment, watching the two men who had become so important to her. Her father looked more relaxed than she'd seen him in years, his face soft with contentment as he gazed at the tree. Beckett worked quietly with the fire, his movements economical and sure. The scene felt like something from a Christmas card, all warm light and peaceful domesticity.

"I'll make us some hot chocolate," she offered, needing something to do with her hands. Dr. Miller's job offer kept circling through her mind.

"That sounds perfect, sweetheart. Use your mother's recipe. Beckett knows where she kept the good cocoa."

The casual way he mentioned her mother's recipe, shared with Beckett but not with her, might have stung weeks ago. Now it felt like another bridge being built, another connection that bound the three of them together in ways she was still learning to appreciate.

In the kitchen, Beckett appeared beside her as she gathered mugs from the cabinet. He reached past her for the tin of cocoa on the high shelf, his arm brushing against hers in the small space. The contact sent warmth spiraling through her that had nothing to do with the heat from the stove.

"Your mother always added a pinch of cinnamon," he said quietly, setting the tin on the counter. "And just a touch of vanilla."

She nodded, afraid to speak, afraid her voice would shake.

"Show me," she said, surprised by the huskiness in her own voice.

He moved behind her, his hands covering hers as he guided her through the measurements. She could feel the warmth of his chest against her back, smell the clean scent of snow and smoke that always seemed to cling to him. When he reached around her to add the cinnamon, she let herself lean back slightly into his solid presence.

"Like this," he murmured, his breath warm against her ear as he helped her stir. "She said the secret was in the stirring. Slow circles, clockwise."

The intimacy of the moment wrapped around them like the steam rising from the pan. She turned in the circle of his arms, finding herself face to face with him in the small kitchen. His eyes searched hers, and she saw her own uncertainty reflected there, mixed with something deeper and more dangerous.

"Tessa," he started, but she shook her head.

"The cocoa will burn," she whispered, though neither of them moved to tend it.

The spell broke when her father called from the living room, asking if they needed help. Beckett stepped back, and she turned to the stove with hands that shook slightly as she finished preparing the drinks.

They returned to the living room with steaming mugs, settling on the couch while her father remained in his chair. The fire crackled peacefully, and the lights on the Christmas tree cast everything in a warm, magical glow. Snow continued to fall outside the windows, cocooning them in their own little world.

"This reminds me of Christmas when you were

little," her father said, his voice soft with memory. "Your mother would make cocoa, and we'd sit by the tree after you'd gone to bed, planning what Santa would bring."

The pain in his voice was gentle now, nostalgic rather than sharp. Healing, she realized. They were all healing in their own ways.

"I have something for you, Dad," she said suddenly, the words slipping out before she could second-guess herself. She'd been carrying the gift in her coat pocket for days, unsure when or if she'd find the courage to give it to him.

She retrieved a small wrapped package from her coat, her heart beating faster as she handed it to him. She hoped it would express feelings she wasn't sure she had words for.

Her father opened his gift. Inside was a small leather photo album, and his breath caught as he opened it to find pictures she'd collected from her childhood, her mother's things, and recent photos from her phone of the three of them decorating the tree.

"Oh, sweetheart," he said, his voice thick. "This is perfect. Look, here's your mother making those cookies with you. And here we are just last week." He traced the edge of a photo with one finger. "A family album. A real family album."

The word family hung in the air, and she felt

peace settle inside her. Yes, she thought. That's exactly what they'd become.

"Well," her father said, his voice gruff with emotion. "I think I'm going to turn in. Leave you young folks to enjoy the fire." He stood, pausing to kiss her forehead. "Thank you for the album. And thank you for coming home."

He squeezed Beckett's shoulder as he passed. "Thank you for everything, son."

Then they were alone, the fire crackling between them and the Christmas tree lights twinkling in the corner. The silence stretched, but it wasn't uncomfortable. It felt full of possibility.

She finally broke the silence. "I have a gift for you, Beckett."

"You don't need to give me anything."

She smiled. "But I want to."

She reached into her pocket and pulled out a small object wrapped in a faded floral handkerchief. She had found it tucked away in her mother's sewing box, a forgotten treasure. Extending her hand, she offered it to him. His gaze dropped to her palm, and he hesitated before taking it, his calloused fingers gentle as they brushed against hers.

He carefully unfolded the cloth. Lying in the center was a small pocket knife, its handle worn smooth and dark with age. It was a simple, elegant thing, made for a smaller hand but clearly well used.

"It was my mother's," she said, her voice quiet in the firelit room. "She kept it in her apron. For cutting twine in the garden, opening letters, whatever she needed."

He ran his thumb over the polished handle, his expression unreadable but reverent. "Tessa, I can't take something so precious."

"You're not taking it. I'm giving it to you." She curled his fingers around the knife. "I know you have your own, but I thought… this one shouldn't be put away in a box anymore. It should belong to someone who understands the value of a good tool."

He looked up then, his gray-blue eyes meeting hers, and in their depths she saw a profound, unspoken gratitude that made her breath catch.

"I'll treasure it always." He set it on the table beside him. "And I have something else for you." He reached into his pocket and pulled out another small package, this one wrapped in tissue paper. "I couldn't decide which one to give you earlier. But this one I wanted to give you when we were alone." He paused, looking uncertain. "This one felt too personal. Too much like hoping for things I didn't have a right to hope for."

Her heart hammered against her ribs as she took the package. Inside was another carved ornament, this one even more delicate than the first. It was a snowflake, intricate and beautiful, with each point and curve carved with exquisite detail. The wood was pale and smooth, and when she held it up to the firelight, the carved patterns created shadows that danced like real frost.

"It's incredible," she breathed. "Beckett, this is art. This is museum-quality work."

He ducked his head, embarrassed by the praise. "I've been working on it for weeks. Every night after you and your dad went to bed, I'd sit in the garage and carve. I kept thinking about you, about how you came back here and changed everything. How you made me believe I could be more than my worst mistake."

She looked up from the ornament to find him watching her intently.

"Each snowflake is different," he continued, his voice soft. "Unique. No two are ever the same. And I thought about how you're like that. One of a kind. And how maybe what we're building here, the three of us, maybe that's unique too. Something that's never existed before."

He paused, taking a shaky breath. "To families that choose each other. To second chances and new beginnings."

The ornament blurred in her vision as tears gathered in her eyes. She set it carefully on the coffee table and looked at him, really looked at him. This man who had been broken by his past but had somehow found the strength to build something beautiful from the pieces. This man who saw her clearly, flaws and fears and all, and chose to carve her gifts that spoke to the deepest parts of her heart.

"Beckett," she whispered.

He leaned forward slightly, his eyes searching her face. "I know I don't have the right to ask for more than friendship. I know my past makes me a risk. But Tessa, these past weeks with you, they've been the best of my life. You make me want to believe in possibilities I thought were lost to me."

She couldn't find words for everything she was feeling. The gratitude, the tenderness, the growing certainty that this man had become essential to her in ways she was still discovering. So instead of speaking, she acted.

She leaned forward and kissed him.

It was soft at first, tentative, a question more than a statement. But when he kissed her back, his hands coming up to frame her face with infinite gentleness, she deepened it. The kiss was slow and careful but certain, full of all the words they hadn't said and all the hope they'd been afraid to voice.

When they finally broke apart, she rested her forehead against his, breathing unsteadily.

"I don't care about your past," she whispered. "I care about who you are now. Who you are with me, with my father, with this town. I care about the man who carves beautiful things in the garage at night and makes hot chocolate with cinnamon because that's how my mother liked it."

His thumb traced across her cheekbone, catching a tear she didn't realize had fallen.

"What about Denver?" he asked quietly. "Your job, your life there?"

She thought about Dr. Miller's offer and about the possibility of staying and building something real and lasting in the place where she'd grown up.

"My life is here now," she said, surprised by the certainty in her own voice. "Maybe it has been all along, and I just needed to find my way back to it."

He kissed her again, and this time there was joy in it, bright and warm as the fire crackling beside them. Outside, snow continued to fall on Sweet River Falls, lovingly covering the town in a blanket of white. Inside, by the Christmas tree and the dying fire, two people who had been lost found their way home to each other.

Dear Reader, thank you for reading my story. I hope it brought you a bit of the magic of the Christmas Season. If you want to read more about Sweet River, try my Sweet River series full of family, friendship, and more of the quaint small-town mountain charm. See more of Annie and Nora.

Oh, and meet Gloria… a troublemaker that rivals my character, Camille, in some of my beach stores.

If you missed the first Christmas Seashells and Snowflakes book, Seaside Christmas Wishes, be sure to grab it for a nice trip back to Belle Island and Lighthouse Point.

As always, thanks for reading my stories. I truly appreciate all my readers. ~Kay

KAY'S BOOKS

Find more information on all my books at ***kaycorrell.com***

Buy direct from Kay's Shop at ***shop.kaycorrell.com***

COMFORT CROSSING ~ THE SERIES

The Shop on Main - Book One

The Memory Box - Book Two

The Christmas Cottage - A Holiday Novella (Book 2.5)

The Letter - Book Three

The Christmas Scarf - A Holiday Novella (Book 3.5)

The Magnolia Cafe - Book Four

The Unexpected Wedding - Book Five

The Wedding in the Grove - (a crossover short story

between series - with Josephine and Paul from The Letter.)

LIGHTHOUSE POINT ~ THE SERIES
Wish Upon a Shell - Book One
Wedding on the Beach - Book Two
Love at the Lighthouse - Book Three
Cottage near the Point - Book Four
Return to the Island - Book Five
Bungalow by the Bay - Book Six
Christmas Comes to Lighthouse Point - Book Seven

CHARMING INN ~ Return to Lighthouse Point
One Simple Wish - Book One
Two of a Kind - Book Two
Three Little Things - Book Three
Four Short Weeks - Book Four
Five Years or So - Book Five
Six Hours Away - Book Six
Charming Christmas - Book Seven

SWEET RIVER ~ THE SERIES
A Dream to Believe in - Book One
A Memory to Cherish - Book Two
A Song to Remember - Book Three
A Time to Forgive - Book Four
A Summer of Secrets - Book Five
A Moment in the Moonlight - Book Six

MOONBEAM BAY ~ THE SERIES

The Parker Women - Book One
The Parker Cafe - Book Two
A Heather Parker Original - Book Three
The Parker Family Secret - Book Four
Grace Parker's Peach Pie - Book Five
The Perks of Being a Parker - Book Six

BLUE HERON COTTAGES ~ THE SERIES

Memories of the Beach - Book One
Walks along the Shore - Book Two
Bookshop near the Coast - Book Three
Restaurant on the Wharf - Book Four
Lilacs by the Sea - Book Five
Flower Shop on Magnolia - Book Six
Christmas by the Bay - Book Seven
Sea Glass from the Past - Book Eight

MAGNOLIA KEY ~ THE SERIES

Saltwater Sunrise - Book One
Encore Echoes - Book Two
Coastal Candlelight - Book Three
Tidal Treasures - Book Four
Bayside Beginnings - Book Five
Seaside Sunshine - Book Six
Boardwalk Breezes - Book Seven

CHRISTMAS SEASHELLS AND SNOWFLAKES

Seaside Christmas Wishes
Sweet River Holiday Homecoming

WIND CHIME BEACH ~ A stand-alone novel

INDIGO BAY ~
Sweet Days by the Bay - Kay's Complete Collection
of stories in the Indigo Bay series

Sign up for my newsletter at my website *kaycorrell.com*
to make sure you don't miss any new releases or
sales.

CHARMING INN ~ Return to Lighthouse Point

One Simple Wish - Book One

Two of a Kind - Book Two

Three Little Things - Book Three

Four Short Weeks - Book Four

Five Years or So - Book Five

Six Hours Away - Book Six

Charming Christmas - Book Seven

SWEET RIVER ~ THE SERIES

A Dream to Believe in - Book One

A Memory to Cherish - Book Two

A Song to Remember - Book Three

A Time to Forgive - Book Four

A Summer of Secrets - Book Five

A Moment in the Moonlight - Book Six

MOONBEAM BAY ~ THE SERIES

The Parker Women - Book One

The Parker Cafe - Book Two

A Heather Parker Original - Book Three

The Parker Family Secret - Book Four

Grace Parker's Peach Pie - Book Five

The Perks of Being a Parker - Book Six

BLUE HERON COTTAGES ~ THE SERIES

Memories of the Beach - Book One

Walks along the Shore - Book Two

Bookshop near the Coast - Book Three

Restaurant on the Wharf - Book Four

Lilacs by the Sea - Book Five

Flower Shop on Magnolia - Book Six

Christmas by the Bay - Book Seven

Sea Glass from the Past - Book Eight

MAGNOLIA KEY ~ THE SERIES

Saltwater Sunrise - Book One

Encore Echoes - Book Two

Coastal Candlelight - Book Three

Tidal Treasures - Book Four

Bayside Beginnings - Book Five

Seaside Sunshine - Book Six

Boardwalk Breezes - Book Seven

CHRISTMAS SEASHELLS AND SNOWFLAKES

Seaside Christmas Wishes

Sweet River Holiday Homecoming

WIND CHIME BEACH ~ A stand-alone novel

INDIGO BAY ~

Sweet Days by the Bay - Kay's complete collection of stories in the Indigo Bay series

ABOUT THE AUTHOR

Kay Correll is a USA Today bestselling author of sweet, heartwarming stories that are a cross between women's fiction and contemporary romance. She is known for her charming small towns, quirky towns-folk, and the enduring strong friendships between the women in her books.

Kay splits her time between the southwest coast of Florida and the Midwest of the U.S. and can often be found out and about with her camera, taking a myriad of photographs, often incorporating them into her book covers. When not lost in her writing or photography, she can be found spending time with her ever-supportive husband, knitting, or playing with her puppies - a cavalier who is too cute for his own good and a naughty but adorable Australian shepherd. Their five boys are all grown now and while she misses the rowdy boy-noise chaos, she is thoroughly enjoying her empty nest years.

Learn more about Kay and her books at kaycorrell.com

While you're there, sign up for her newsletter to hear about new releases, sales, and giveaways.

WHERE TO FIND ME:
My shop: shop.kaycorrell.com
My author website: kaycorrell.com
authorcontact@kaycorrell.com

Join my Facebook Reader Group. We have lots of fun and you'll hear about sales and new releases first!
www.facebook.com/groups/KayCorrell/

I love to hear from my readers. Feel free to contact me at authorcontact@kaycorrell.com

facebook.com/KayCorrellAuthor

instagram.com/kaycorrell

pinterest.com/kaycorrellauthor

amazon.com/author/kaycorrell

bookbub.com/authors/kay-correll

9 781966 284192